# TOO YOUNG TO DIE IN THE GARDEN OF SYN

## MICHAEL SEIDELMAN

Book Three In THE GARDEN OF SYN Trilogy

Chewed
Pencil
Press

*Dedicated to the cystic fibrosis community
and those tirelessly fighting for a cure*

Prologue

# A Stranger is Watching

For as long as Synthia Wade can remember, she often felt like someone was watching her. Syn thought that maybe she was being paranoid. But the truth of the matter was, for most of her life she *was* being watched.

The Stranger had been shadowing Syn's house since Syn was only five years old. It began a few weeks after her parents went missing. No one knew what had happened to Ian and Debra Wade. Almost no one.

The Stranger knew. Not only did she know, but more than anything, she wanted to join them.

If Syn's parents had not vanished they would have had many memories of their daughter, good and bad: her first day of school, birthday parties in their beautiful garden, and the worsening of the illness that sent her to the hospital far too often. But Syn's parents did not experience these events and thus, have no memories of them.

The Stranger, on the other hand, remembers them all. While lurking in the daylight or hiding in the shadows of the night, she watched Syn grow up to become a brave young woman.

The Stranger saw Syn's first kiss down by the pond with that boy, Jonathan. The very same spot where soon after, a hooded teenager pushed Syn into the water. She sank and did not return to the surface.

Most would be horrified by such a sight, but the Stranger was thrilled because it gave her hope for the first time in many years. The young man removed his hood to reveal two faces, and the Stranger excitedly watched him follow Syn into the pond and disappear. It was happening. Finally.

The Stranger went to her rented cabin on a nearby property and wrote a message to the others. She told them that there was activity and that she would report back soon. She placed the piece of paper under what looked like a desk lamp, hit a button, and a stream of light shot out. When the light disappeared, the note was gone.

When Syn reappeared a week later, she was floating face down on the surface of the pond. The Stranger turned her over and saved her life, before running from the scene. A police officer found her moments later.

The Stranger was disappointed. No, bitter. Because the girl was alone.

Back to square one.

While Syn spent time in the hospital, the Stranger watched the camera feed of her house from the monitor in her cabin.

She watched.

She waited.

One night, the boy with two faces appeared again, seemingly out of nowhere, at the back of Syn's garden. He held two young men at gunpoint, forcing them to carry boxes and equipment from a truck parked on the street to the back of Syn's garden. Back and forth they went. When the two-faced boy reappeared, carrying the body of one of his hostages, the Stranger watched him hide the body on a neighboring farm.

That was not the last time she saw the presumed killer. He visited a few times, peeking into windows at the Wade house and watching from behind a bush, unaware that he was also being watched.

One night, Syn snuck out and met up with two of her friends. She vanished, and her friends followed shortly after. Days passed and the Stranger witnessed no new activity. She was losing hope, until they finally returned home with a girl she had never seen before. This girl resembled Syn when she was younger.

Now *this* was interesting.

Months passed and whenever the Stranger saw Syn, the young girl she called Beth was always by her side. She knew they must be sisters. Fascinating. Though her unsatisfied curiosity about what they were up to and why, was maddening.

Then one day, *she* appeared. Debra Wade, in the flesh. Waiting for this moment was the Stranger's sole purpose. Any thoughts about having wasted years of her life were vanquished.

The Stranger returned to her cabin and threw a metal disc on the wood-panelled floor. She was ready for the beam of light that streaked to the ceiling, promptly stepping into it and disappearing.

It was time to alert the others.

Chapter 1

# THE DEVIL YOU KNOW

*JUST BREATHE.*

*Just breathe*, I tell myself again. I've been here before. Betrayed by the people I loved and trusted the most. The boy I had feelings for ended up being a monster who was baiting me for a dangerous trap. My own parents, whose return I yearned for, were monsters too, torturing and murdering girls just like myself and killing countless people in other worlds.

Those betrayals shook me to the core. And, discovering that my parents had not only done horrific things, but that they had done so for me, was devastating. However, *this. This* somehow is even worse.

Aunt Ruth, my mom's sister, had taken care of me ever since I was five. Ever since my parents' research partner Masie Winters had trapped them in the Garden. Or so I thought.

Now my mother has escaped her long captivity in the Garden and has beaten the truth out of my caregiver. She isn't even my mom's sister. She isn't even my aunt. I pleaded with her to tell me her real name and her answer will haunt me forever: Masie Winters.

I'm feeling numb and telling myself to breathe, though I should calm my breathing. I'm hyperventilating. Am I having a panic attack? The oxygen tank is right beside me. Is it not working?! Everything goes quiet except for the swirling, incoherent thoughts inside my head. Finally, one voice breaks through.

"Syn?" My eleven-year-old sister is concerned. "Just breathe." Beth repeats what I just told myself. "Breathe slowly." She takes my arm but I don't feel her touch.

Mom is holding Masie by her throat, oblivious to my condition. Masie's eyes don't show the expression of an evil person whose plan has gone awry, they show sorrow.

"Where is my sister?" Mom demands. "Did you kill her?"

Masie is watching me. My former caregiver knows that she's breaking my heart and it's eating away at her.

"Did you kill my sister?" Mom screams in her ear, still gripping her throat.

Masie nods.

Mom smashes Masie's face against the table, knocking her unconscious and letting her collapse onto the kitchen floor.

The room begins to spin and I sink to my knees. Everything is blurry. Faint echoes of Mom and Beth calling my name are the last thing I remember before everything goes black.

* * *

My eyelids feel like concrete slabs and I must tighten my muscles to lift them. I'm lying on the couch in the living room. The lights are off but the room is illuminated through the white curtains that hang on the closed glass French doors leading to the kitchen. The mild aroma of Chinese takeout that wafts into the room is comforting, until my mind clears and the events that preceded my slumber send a jolt through my body.

In a panic, I disconnect myself from the oxygen tank and leap off the couch. When I fling open both kitchen doors, the back of Masie's head is the first thing that greets me. Her body is slumped in a chair at the table. Her hands are tied behind the chair and her ankles are bound by rope.

Beth is sitting opposite Masie, casually slurping chow mein. Open boxes of dim sum are strewn across the table.

As soon as Beth sees me she scoots off her chair and runs to me with outstretched arms. "Are you okay?"

I study the unconscious Masie closely. "Where's Mom?"

Beth points to the basement door. The clock above it reads 8:08. "You've been out for more than two hours. You should eat something."

"I'm not hungry."

"You have to eat," Beth insists.

She's right. With cystic fibrosis, I have to keep my calorie count high, especially since I'm on the waiting list for a lung transplant. My health must be maintained or I'll be bumped down the list, or booted off altogether.

Masie has remained as still as a statue, except for the slight rise and fall of her chest.

"We can eat in the living room," Beth says. "Away from…"

"No. I want her to be right in front of me."

I sit down at the table, and study the woman who was more of a mother to me than my real mother ever was. She and Beth were my world. None of this makes any sense. It's like looking at puzzle pieces and not knowing how they fit together.

Beth notices I'm not eating and places food from each container onto my plate.

I pick up a wonton with my chopsticks and shove it into my mouth.

"You feeling okay?"

I shrug.

"This whole thing is crazy," Beth says. "I'm mad at myself for not realizing who she was."

"There's no way you could have known. I didn't even know."

"I sensed something when I first met her but she seemed so genuine, so I let it go. It was obvious she loved you and I think she was even beginning to love me."

"She didn't love either of us." I swallow bitterness along with my wonton. "It was an elaborate ruse. Revenge."

"No."

The sound of Masie's voice is startling. I jump up and my chair falls backwards.

"I always loved you." She speaks slowly, in a stupor.

Stomping footsteps quickly ascend the basement stairs and the door bursts open. Mom makes certain that I'm fine, and then punches Masie square in the nose.

"Mom!"

Blood is dripping from Masie's nose and she's out cold again.

"That bitch killed my sister, and raised you while holding your father and me captive in the Garden."

"I know. Think of how I feel. I loved her like a mother."

The sting in Mom's eyes is evident. She brushes a strand of hair away from my eyes.

I shove her away. "Move Masie to my room."

Mom is perplexed.

"I have questions that only my...Masie...can answer."

"We all do, Syn. Like how she has been around town claiming to be my sister, with not one person recognizing her as Masie."

"Masie kind of looks like Aunt Ruth," Beth interjects, handing over her phone with a Google image search of Masie Winters onscreen.

Of course the photos had been altered. They don't look exactly like the woman tied up in our kitchen, with altered hairstyle and different glasses. They are sort of a halfway point between Masie and Aunt Ruth. Anyone who saw photos on Masie's university faculty page or in her fake obituary would see someone similar to the woman they knew. Plus, when I Googled Masie Winters over the years, the woman looked different enough from the photos I'd seen of my aunt that I wouldn't think too much of it.

"But you met your aunt and Masie when you were a girl."

"Mom, I don't remember meeting Aunt Ruth. I was what, two?" My voice is breaking up. Tears are filling my eyes. "I remember being introduced to Masie briefly, but not what she looked like then, any more than your other colleagues. Your sister hadn't lived in Redfern since she was a teenager and that was more than twenty years ago."

Mom is exasperated. "You have a lot of questions, but I will talk to her first."

Tears of frustration are streaming down my face. "There are so many questions to ask. I want to understand."

"We can question her together."

"Together? From the minute you came into this house my life has been torn apart. She raised me, Mom."

"She doesn't love you."

"Yes, she does." Beth's voice is firm. Her hand is soft on my back, helping me to relax, just a little.

"Please move her to my room. I want to talk to her alone. My whole world has fallen apart."

There's a moment of silence while Mom studies Masie's slouched form and my tear-stained face.

"Fine, I'll take her upstairs. But if you help her escape, I swear I'll find her and kill her."

"You think I'd let her go? She murdered Aunt Ruth and raised me while pretending to be her. The last thing I want is for her to get away."

"Meet me in your room after you've finished everything on your plate." Mom begins to drag Masie's chair to the stairs.

Masie's eyes fly open in a panic. "Syn, I know you're confused, but listen to me. You and your family are in terrible danger!"

Mom takes a cloth napkin from the table and shoves it into Masie's mouth, then carries her up the stairs, Masie mumbling the whole way.

"Terrible danger? What was that all about?" Beth asks.

"I have no idea. But I'll find out soon enough."

# Chapter 2

# SOMETHING WICKED THIS WAY COMES

BETH AND I ARE SITTING on my bed across from Masie, who's still gagged and tied to the chair.

"Beth…"

"You'd like to talk to her alone." Beth is reading my mind.

"I know she lied to you too, but…"

"She was with you most of your life. Mom's downstairs and I'll be in my room. Just yell if you need us." Beth double-checks the ropes that bind our prisoner, and exits the room.

I'm alone with the Aunt Ruth imposter—the woman who killed my real aunt and pretended to care about me. I look into Masie's eyes and shiver, despite the room being warm. She is desperate to speak. I remove the gag.

"I know you have questions, but—"

"Shut up!"

"Listen. You are in terrible danger."

"Enough."

I stuff the napkin back into her mouth and take a couple of seconds to calm myself. "Okay. This is how this is going to work. You will answer my questions. All of them. Then, and only then, can you tell me about this *so-called* danger."

Masie isn't ready to play ball.

"Or, I can just leave you here." I march to the door and rest a hand on the doorknob, glancing over my shoulder. "Yeah, think I'll go watch some Netflix."

Masie squirms.

I open the door slowly. "We can try this again in a couple of hours."

After a beat, she nods.

I close the door and scrutinize Masie's eyes, trying not to crumble. "Not a word of that danger garbage until you answer all my questions." I remove her gag.

She is desperate to say something, opens her mouth to speak, but stops herself when a tear slides down my cheek.

"I…I don't get it." I'm shaking. "Were you just pretending to love me?"

"No, Syn. I do love you."

"You trapped my parents in the Garden. You killed my aunt."

"Yes."

"You pretended to be Ruth Lowery."

"Yes," she responds, sounding remorseful.

"How am I supposed to believe that you love me? You did those terrible things for what…revenge?"

"Revenge." Masie speaks as if she doesn't like the way the word lifts off her tongue. "Yes, I suppose. At first, I was angry. I had worked hard on something and made a breakthrough no scientist on our planet had ever achieved. Not only had I proven that the multiverse existed, I could travel between worlds and even create new ones. It was all based on a fluke. One of many trials I could never duplicate without my research—my data.

"Your parents asked to use my findings because they wanted me to help them create a cure for illness. For you. That wasn't my goal. Their goal was admirable; however, they wanted to do things that were beyond my moral capacity to accept. Terrible things, Syn. I refused and your parents took everything. They locked me out of a world I created. They took every bit of research and data that mattered and left me with nothing. No family. No friends. This breakthrough was everything to me and I had great aspirations for it. I wanted to better the world with my discoveries in a way that wouldn't use human beings as lab rats. I was furious."

"You wanted revenge."

"I suppose that is the correct word then. Yes, I craved revenge."

"So, you trapped my parents in the Garden, killed my aunt and replaced her, and became my guardian. What was the plan?"

"I…didn't have much of a plan. Your parents loved you more than anything. So much, that they would shut me out in an attempt to find a cure for your CF. If I'm being honest with myself, keeping them from a daughter they loved more than anything else seemed like the perfect revenge."

"Were you going to kill me? Inherit my family's money?"

"Never. I couldn't care less about your parents' money. I refused to share my findings with your parents because of their plan to use alternate versions of you as guinea pigs. That idea was abhorrent."

"Kinda like the pot calling the kettle black."

She doesn't argue that.

"What was your plan for me?"

"There was no plan. I never wanted a kid, and honestly didn't know what to do with you after being granted guardianship."

"I was in the way. So you didn't love me." I swallowed against the lump in my throat.

"Not at first. I would watch you and wonder what the hell I was doing. Shortly after I moved into this house though, you got very sick."

"I remember."

"You were coughing and wheezing and barely able to breathe. I was heartbroken. Something changed. Perhaps I was feeling like a mother holding her child for the first time. But the truth was that I loved you and hated seeing you suffer. You weren't mine to lose, but I was still afraid to lose you. Maybe it was guilt from keeping your parents from you."

"So you felt like you owed it to me. That you should care for me to make up for what you did."

"It was more than just guilt. When I spent time in the hospital with you, I was terrified that you wouldn't make it. From that day on, I loved you like you were my daughter. I could not undo what had been done, being locked out of the Garden. So yes, I owed it to you to give you everything after taking away so much. It went beyond obligation. It was love."

Tears are streaming down Masie's cheeks. I'm a weeping mess too. I've questioned Masie's sincerity, but when I think back to all those years—even my angsty teen years—she was always there for me. She never missed a school event. She stayed up all night with me when I was sick, and even became president of our local cystic fibrosis support group chapter. I remember her telling me how much she loved me. Deep in my heart, I knew she meant it. And when Beth came along, Masie treated her like she was her own.

"Syn, I would do anything for you and Beth. I would die for you both."

I reach for Masie and hug her tightly. She has done horrible things, but there is no doubt about her love for me. She truly would die for me. I relate to that feeling from when Beth's life was in jeopardy and I was ready to do whatever it took to protect her.

Masie killed my aunt, an innocent human being who had hurt no one. Yet as much as it hurts and regardless of the unforgivable act of murder, I will never fully accept that the woman in front of me is Masie Winters. She'll always be Aunt Ruth to me.

"Syn." Aunt Ruth's teary voice is muffled by my hair.

I pull away to listen.

"I really need to tell you—"

The door flies open and Beth sweeps in. Her eyes dart to Aunt Ruth for only a moment as she races to the window. "Look!"

I have a sudden feeling of déjà vu as I hurry to the window. Three figures are lurking in the evening shadows, facing our house. They are completely still, with identical outlines and standing equal distance to each other, like paper doll cut-outs.

"They're here," Aunt Ruth says. "This is what I needed to warn you about."

I squint to make out their faces and turn to Beth with wide eyes. Each one resembles Aunt Ruth. All three figures are Masie Winters.

# Chapter 3

# SHOT THROUGH THE HEART

*THREE MORE MASIES?*

"There are two more in the backyard," Beth says.

*What the hell is happening?*

"Okay, Winters," says Beth. "Talk."

"They want your mother. And they will use both of you as leverage to get to her."

"I'm so confused." I comb my fingers through my hair.

"Beth, tell your mother to gather as many weapons as she can."

Beth looks at me for approval.

"Do it."

She darts into the hallway and I listen to her thumping down the stairs.

"What do you see out there now?"

"There are more Masies than there were just a minute ago."

"How many?"

"Five."

"You have to untie me. So I can help."

*Can I trust her, despite everything?*

"Listen, Syn. I have been preparing for this day for years, and can't protect you while I'm tied to this chair."

"Fine. But you have to tell me what's happening." I begin to fumble with the knot around her wrists.

*Mom did a real job on this.*

"You already know that I trapped your parents in the Garden they created. Well, in a different world, another version of me who experienced a similar betrayal murdered your parents from that world. After they were dead, this other me came up with a plan but had to get into the Garden to execute it. However, she essentially threw away the key when she killed your parents."

I am close to untying the knot when it hits me. If my parents betrayed Masie in another world, would that mean there is another Garden?

"This other me jumped from world to world, recruiting more versions of us to help her with her plan. She built an army."

I finally untie the knot.

"These women want more than just revenge." Aunt Ruth begins to untie her ankles. "They want to get into the Garden and will do anything to succeed. They've been watching this house for years. Watching you and waiting for your parents to come back."

Aunt Ruth is almost free.

"Now that your mother has returned, they've mobilized. They will use you and your sister to force her hand and let them into the Garden."

The ropes fall away from Aunt Ruth's feet and we race to the window. My feeling of déjà vu returns. There are twelve Masies now. The figures begin to move towards the house.

There's banging on the front door. They're trying to kick it in!

Aunt Ruth takes my arm and we meet Mom and Beth at the bedroom door. Mom is pointing a gun at Aunt Ruth.

"Mom," I plead. "Don't."

Both the front and back door have been smashed in now. I dare to peek into the hallway. A herd of Masie Winters is stomping up the stairs.

"What the hell?" Mom mumbles in disbelief.

As they reach the top of the stairs, Mom fires twice. They keep coming. She slams my door closed and helps Aunt Ruth push my dresser against it. We all lean against the dresser as angry Masies hurl themselves against the door.

"What is this?" Mom shrieks.

"They want to get into the Garden. They will take your children hostage to force your hand. We can't let that happen."

We aren't strong enough to hold them off. There are too many of them. The dresser gradually inches across the carpet, allowing the door to crack open farther.

"Debra," Aunt Ruth shouts above the noise in the hallway, "I had planned a way out, but didn't have enough time."

*Because she was tied up and I wouldn't let her tell me about the danger until I got answers.*

"I hoped it wouldn't come to this, but I can't think of another way for you and the girls to escape."

"We can shoot them," Beth says. She holds up a gun Mom must've given her.

"How many bullets do you have, Debra?" Aunt Ruth asks.

"These two guns are loaded. That's it."

"That won't be enough. There are too many of them."

An arm reaches through the crack in the doorway.

"What's your plan?" Mom shouts.

Aunt Ruth takes Mom's wrist and shoves the muzzle of the gun against her chest. "Right in the heart. Now!"

"No!" I scream.

More arms are reaching through the doorway and the dresser inches farther forward.

"What kind of plan is that?" I yell. "How the hell will that help us?"

"You have to do it, Debra," Aunt Ruth says. She turns to me. "Synthia, I'm sorry for everything. Always know that I—"

BLAM!

I scream as the blast shakes my room. Aunt Ruth falls to the floor, blood seeping from the hole in her chest.

# Chapter 4

# THE GREAT ESCAPE

I DROP TO THE FLOOR by Aunt Ruth's side. Her glassy eyes are staring at the ceiling.

"Mom, what did you do?!"

"What she told me to." Mom pulls me off the floor while Beth watches sadly.

The dresser continues to jerk across the carpet as bodies crash against it, and the door opens wider. Mom uses the butt of her gun to whack fingers that are gripping the edge of the door.

"Why?" I plead, mucus funneling its way into my lungs as I weep for Aunt Ruth. "What good did this do? She's dead and we're still trapped."

"Look!" Beth is pointing to Aunt Ruth. There's a red glow protruding from the hole in her chest.

Mom pushes past us and drops to her knees. "I'm sorry about this, girls." She reaches into the bloody hole in Ruth's chest and pries apart the flesh. Blood gushes everywhere. But that's not the only thing. A bold stream of red light beams from Aunt Ruth's chest to the ceiling.

A lightway. A *red* lightway!

"Go girls! I'll be right behind you."

Beth goes first. She puts one foot on either side of Aunt Ruth's body and all movement halts. Her form fades into the red illumination.

I whisper goodbye to my aunt. My tears freeze like the rest of my body when I step into the light. The dresser is shoved over and the door bursts open. I'm unable to move as the lightway works its magic, fading me from my room, which used to be a safe place.

Mom shoots several Masies. As the red glow brightens, the last thing I see is Mom running towards me. Another bullet is flying from her gun into the chest of a woman who looks just like the woman who raised me.

* * *

I can move again… and am still in my bedroom? Beth is here. Unfamiliar pictures are hanging on the walls and the dresser is back in its rightful spot. Aunt Ruth's body is gone, as is the red lightway.

The door is wide open and there's no one trying to get in. And, oh…another me…another Syn?…is sitting on the bed, wearing flannel pajama bottoms with a loose t-shirt and a physical therapy vest. This isn't my bedroom. It's hers.

The other Syn is gaping at us. The physical therapy vest is humming as it shakes fluid loose in her lungs.

Mom appears beside me, followed by one Masie. Mom shoots Masie in the head. Blood spurts onto the window behind her and Masie slumps to the floor. The other Syn doesn't move, confused and petrified.

"It will be okay," I tell her, aware that was unlikely. Nothing ever seems to be okay in my life. Why should it be any different in hers?

Mom glances around the room and out the door into the hallway. Another Masie appears, then another. Mom shoots them both.

"Follow me," Mom says. "We have to find another lightway."

We run back and forth across the hallway, peering into every room and finding nothing.

"Downstairs," Mom orders.

We halt in our tracks before reaching the bottom. Standing there, looking panicked from the gunshots, and now at the sight of us, is my mom's other and my late alt-father.

"Go to your daughter's room," Mom tells them. "Kill anyone who shouldn't be here."

"Except us," Beth adds.

They charge up the stairs to check on their Syn, and we continue our frantic search for a lightway. There was nothing to find in the living room or kitchen, so Mom and I wait at the basement door while Beth tiptoes down the stairs.

Her footsteps slow, and stop. Her excitement is evident when she calls for us. There in the center of the basement is the lightway we've been searching for. It glows red like the one we came through.

"This should take us home. Gather up anything that can be used as a weapon," says Mom. "We will have to fight our way past more of those monsters."

The basement layout matches ours, but the contents are different: tools, lab equipment, a battered recliner, and a fold-out bed. No old computers. No boxes of files.

I don't know what to take, but Beth and Mom are on top of it. Beth grabs a letter opener from a mug that's being used as a pencil holder, and breaks two legs off a folding table.

Mom tries different combinations on a safe in the corner of the room. The safe door opens on her fifth attempt. She takes out two guns and some ammo, reloads her gun, and pockets the extra ammo just as another Masie appears on the staircase. Mom shoots her in the chest. She tumbles down the stairs, hitting her head at the bottom.

"Listen, girls," Mom says, placing a hand on each of our shoulders. "We have a lot to talk about. But for now, we need to return home and make it to the lightway outside. The Garden is the only place Masie Winters can't follow us. Understand?"

Beth and I nod. There is so much I want to say, but no time to waste.

Mom hands Beth another gun. Beth cocks the hammer like she's a trained mercenary. I hate that my little sister is so good with a gun, but acknowledge that her skills might save our lives.

"Let's go," says Mom.

I raise one of the table legs behind my head, ready to strike if necessary. Together, we all step into the light and phase from the red glow into the basement of our own house.

We are greeted by six women who share the name Masie Winters.

# Chapter 5

# IN COLD PURSUIT

TWO MASIES ARE WAITING AT the bottom of the stairs and four are descending behind them. Mom and Beth aim their guns.

"Don't move!"

The women halt at Mom's order.

"Big mistake coming here empty handed," Beth says.

"Why would we have weapons? We aren't here to hurt you."

*Riiiight.*

Mom taps a heel against a stack of storage boxes and whispers, "The big box behind these. 9667."

Behind the storage boxes is indeed a larger storage box. While Mom keeps an eye on the Masies, Beth and I slide the box out from under the table and rip one side open. The box contains a black safe.

"What was the number…?" I stop to cough and clear my throat.

Luckily, my brainy little sister remembers. Beth quickly enters 9667 on the digital keypad. The safe door clicks open just as I hear a whack and a thud.

Someone grabs my legs. I'm dragged past Mom, who is lying on the floor. She's conscious, but dazed.

Beth shoots the Masie who is dragging me. Masie yelps and collapses, gripping her kneecap. Meanwhile, Beth helps Mom up from the floor.

Mom staggers, then aims her gun at our enemies. "Get everything from the safe," she says, keeping her eyes on the Masies. "Quickly!"

Beth races to help me. The safe contains two handguns, several boxes of ammo, two grenades, four flashlights, an assortment of batteries, a backpack, and two tear gas canisters. We toss everything into the backpack.

"Well, ladies," Mom says nonchalantly. "If you don't move out of our way, I'll shoot all of you. My daughter may be merciful, but I won't be aiming for your kneecaps."

The identical women smartly decide to head back upstairs, abandoning the Masie with the wounded knee.

Mom rummages through the backpack and pulls out one of the canisters. She hands each of us a flashlight. "We're gonna escape through the back door. As soon as you're outside make a beeline for the shed."

Beth shrugs into the backpack straps and presses her foot on Masie's bloody knee, causing her to flinch, before leaping onto the staircase.

I raise my eyebrows.

"Oops," she says, smirking.

Mom leads us upstairs, cautiously. We pause at the top, glancing in every direction, and at each other. There are a dozen Masies in the kitchen and foyer, blocking the front and back doors.

Beth aims her gun at the group by the front door.

"You gonna let us through?" Mom snidely asks, waving her gun at the group by the back door.

One of them opens the back door and the group parts like the Red Sea.

Mom leads the way. As we cautiously walk between the Masies to the door, one of them grabs me. Mom shoots my attacker in the center of her forehead and shoves me outside into the cold. I hear four more gunshots before Mom and Beth join me.

Mom pulls the tip off the tear gas canister and chucks it into the house. "Run!"

We stomp down the icy stairs, Mom catching me twice as I slip. I am shivering. It's a chilly winter night and we aren't dressed properly. I have difficulty breathing the cold air.

We run to the garden, past four more Masies. They move out of the way when Mom fires a warning shot.

Mom leads us past the pond to the back of our property, where trees, hedges, and bushes provide ample hiding spots in close proximity to the shed. I can make out at least ten figures surrounding the structure.

"Mom, how do they know that's where we're going? They shouldn't be able to see the lightway if they're blocked from the Garden."

"I don't know."

"What's the plan?" Beth asks.

I know from my adventures with Beth in the Garden that it's likely she already came up with her own plan, but she defers to Mom's lead.

Mom brings us back in the direction we came and stops in front of the pond. The coast is clear so far, but there are still Masies searching for us.

"Both of you hide in those bushes."

"What are you going to do?"

Mom hands her gun to Beth. "Just do what I say."

She waits until we are hidden, then sits down and slips her feet into the freezing water. We both gasp as Mom slides beneath the surface.

"She obviously has a plan." Beth is trying to reassure me, and likely herself.

My confusion is overwhelming. As seconds become minutes, with no sign of Mom resurfacing, confusion is overcome by fear.

"Enough waiting," Beth says impatiently. "I'm going in."

Suddenly, Mom's head pops out of the water. She's gasping for air.

"Mom!"

The water is only as high as Mom's hips now. The pond is somehow…draining?

"You girls need to get in the water. Now. Before they spot us."

I've never felt cold like this. It numbs my body till I can barely breathe. Mom holds us as the water level rapidly descends. Less than a minute later, the water is ankle deep and we are standing on the uneven muddy surface of the pond amidst lily pads and algae.

My teeth are chattering. I have to work hard to hold the flashlight with numb fingers. Beth's lips are turning blue. She's clutching her gun by her side and water is streaming from her backpack. Mom is oblivious, watching every direction to make sure we are still alone.

"Okay." She points to a half-oval opening in the pond bank.

A concrete slab is lying in front of it like a floor mat. Beyond the opening, a pitch-black tunnel leads into a haunting abyss.

# Chapter 6

# PROHIBITION POND

I HAVE RELAXED BY THIS pond on countless sunny afternoons, dipping my feet into the warm water, none the wiser about the secret hatch that when opened would drain the water.

*Why is there a tunnel? Where does it lead?*

There isn't time to contemplate. Two Masies are looming above us.

"We found them!"

Mom pulls us into the tunnel. Her hands are as cold as ice.

With great difficulty, I turn on the flashlight and see that we're inside a tunnel with corridors constructed of jagged rock. We're wading through shallow pools of water. This place is not that different from the sewers in the Garden, except that here there are no cobwebs, mouse droppings, or any other signs of life.

The silence is short-lived though. Footsteps are splashing through the water behind us. Still struggling with numb fingers, I aim my flashlight carefully, trying not to drop it.

"They're gaining on us," Beth says.

"We have an advantage," Mom says. "I know these tunnels well. Your great-grandparents built them nearly a century ago to smuggle liquor down the river during Prohibition. Your dad and I used these tunnels to set up a back door of sorts to the Garden."

The footsteps are closer, and there are a lot of them.

"Mom, what do we do now?"

Mom takes my flashlight and shines the light above our heads. She slides her free hand across the top of several jagged rocks that are jutting from the side of the tunnel.

"We should keep moving, Mom," says Beth impatiently.

"Hang on a sec."

"Too late," I say.

Two Masies have appeared, and there are more footsteps behind them. Mom finally finds what she's looking for and hands my flashlight back. I shine the light on our enemies. Beth aims her gun at one, then the other.

"Yes, we see the gun, little girl. But there are more of us and you can only shoot one at a time."

The group's chuckling echoes off the walls.

Beth waves her gun at them again. "What do you want?"

"Take us to the Garden."

Mom cocks the gun hammer and the spark lights the wick of the stick of dynamite she just retrieved. "Run!"

She hurls the sizzling stick of dynamite at the Masies and dashes after us. One Masie leaps forward, grabbing Beth's leg and slamming her to the concrete.

"No!" I shout.

BOOM!

The tunnel shakes like we're having an earthquake. A crack breaks across the ceiling, unleashing an avalanche of debris onto our enemies. I run to Beth, coughing as dust fills my lungs.

Her leg is still in the clutches of her attacker. Masie's body is covered with debris, aside from the arm that's attached to Beth's leg.

Mom and I help Beth off the concrete. Besides wet clothes and scrapes, she is fine.

"That was too close for comfort."

"But we all made it." I squeeze her arm.

"We will be okay, girls, now that the tunnel is blocked. They won't be able to get through any time soon."

"I promised myself that I would never go back to the Garden after what all those people went through because of me."

"I say this with love, Syn," Mom says, "but you really need to get over yourself."

That stings. "What do you mean?"

"We're running for our lives and you are still blaming yourself for things that weren't your fault."

She is at least partly right. We are running for our lives. The Garden is the only safe place right now.

"You won't recognize this part of the Garden. It was created by Masie before your father and I were even aware of her breakthrough. It's a part of the same world, but distant enough that the healing properties aren't as strong. You will feel better, Syn. Your symptoms will take much less of a toll than they would at home. But I must tell you that unlike the Garden you know, you can die from a deep flesh wound in this place. We have to be extra careful."

"What is there in this part of the Garden that might hurt us? Creepers?"

"One in particular, I'm afraid. Your father and I first tested transferring life-forms from one world to another in this test site of Masie's. We failed, hence more animal hybrids."

*So what else is new?*

"The part of the Garden you are familiar with has Creepers that share the DNA of two beings. However, during our first test, every animal we attempted to transfer to the Garden was amalgamated into a single creature. A mammoth beast larger and more formidable than any Creeper you have met."

"No, no, no." Beth shivers. "You can't be serious."

*A beast.*

This is what Beth told me roamed in a valley on the other side of the voltway in the Garden sewers. A horrible beast so deadly it scares the bejesus out of a girl who usually fears nothing.

As if on cue, the voltway appears in front of us, just as I remember from that day down in the sewers—a formidable black lightway with yellow and blue crackling electrical currents encircling it. Now we will have to face this beast head-on.

*Dammit, Mom.*

# Chapter 7

# WELCOME TO DEATH VALLEY

"NO, MOM," Beth pleads.

"You've been there? You've seen the beast?"

Beth nods.

Mom rests her hands on Beth's shoulders. "It's nighttime. The creature is sleeping. We're fine as long as we don't wake it."

"And if we do?" I ask.

"There's a steep, rugged hill on the far side of the valley. It's a ten-minute walk, and the sound of the waterfall will lead us there. The beast can't get good footing on the hill, so we can sleep safely up there. We'll make our way to the Garden in the morning."

"When the thing is awake?" Beth asks.

"There is another voltway in the valley that will take us to the Garden. We can't see the voltway in the dark though."

"Can we get there through the fog, like Beth did?"

"That would take a week or longer. We have nothing to eat or drink."

"Beth's right," Mom says. "We have no choice. Just hold my hand and be as quiet as possible. The creatures you'll see scurrying around are harmless."

"More creatures?"

"The beast is a hermaphrodite. It impregnates itself."

"Ew." I feel nauseous.

"Whatever creatures are out there are just its offspring, which it eats once they are fully grown."

"Double ew."

"The food chain is a natural part of the ecosystem, Synthia."

I can't believe Mom refers to her hybrid Frankenstein monster as *natural*.

"The Masies are bound to get through the rubble soon," Mom says. "Follow me. I won't let anything happen to either of you."

She steps into the dark portal and the electrical currents speed up and crackle louder than before.

When they calm down, Beth does her best to smile, and steps forward. "See you on the other side."

Once the currents slow down, I take a deep breath and move into the darkness. This isn't the Garden, or the valley.

I'm not certain I am *anywhere.*

Everything is black. Not the actual color *black,* just pitch-black nothingness. Like when I fell through the abyss in Doom World—the Oblivion. I am not falling this time. I am not breathing either, and that seems to be fine. I'm unable to move my head and can't feel any part of my body. I may not even have a body in this place. There is no sound other than the ability to hear my thoughts. My consciousness seems to be the only thing that exists.

Slowly, I am able to make out an image that's forming in front of me. It's me. With Masie.

*My* Masie. *Aunt Ruth.*

*We are in the Garden. I lean close to tell her something. She looks terribly concerned.*

When I fell through the Oblivion months ago, I had this same vision. It was one of many visions I had while falling. Some were of real-life memories, such as the last time I saw my parents before they disappeared. My first kiss. Meeting Beth. Some visions were of things that never happened. It dawns on me that one of those non-events came to be, just hours ago.

*A dozen shadowy figures standing outside my house at night.*

This means that when I fell through the Oblivion, I saw glimpses of my past and my future. But how can I experience this with Aunt Ruth in the future if she is dead?

Suddenly, I am back in the real world with Mom and Beth. Not the *real* world, the one Masie created. I feel better already. Not perfect, but pretty darn good.

It's nearly pitch-black, but warm like a summer night. Way better than the chilly winter night we just escaped.

A powerful waterfall is thundering in the distance. There is a smoky smell in the air that tickles my throat. Through the darkness, there is a faint orange glow from what must be the top of the hill we're about to climb. Has someone built a small fire?

"Is someone else here?"

"I didn't see anyone when I was here," Beth says. "But I wasn't here long."

There is rustling in nearby bushes.

"Don't worry, everything's fine," says Mom.

She makes sure the gun is still tucked into her pocket. Then we all move forward, hand in hand.

"Same plan," she says. "We head to the hill because that's where we will be safe. We'll deal with whoever is up there in due time."

As we creep across the grass and between bushes, the last few hours all come rushing back to me. We were just about to go out for dinner to celebrate the news about me making the transplant list, Mom arrived, and chaos quickly followed. Just a few hours ago, my Aunt Ruth was my Aunt Ruth. Not a traitor, and certainly not dead. Mom killed her before she could even finish telling me she loved me.

A droplet of mist tickles my face. The waterfall is nearby. I shine my flashlight in that direction hoping to catch a glimpse, but thick shrubbery is blocking the view. As we approach the hill, I notice reflections of the moon and stars on the surface of a lake. Magical. We carefully climb the steep hill in the direction of the campfire.

Mom lets go of my hand near the top and reaches for her gun. The smoke is invading my lungs and I cannot suppress my coughing.

When we reach the top of the hill the campfire is in clear view, but the area is deserted. Mom and Beth are ready to shoot anyone or anything that pounces at us from the shadows. But whoever started this fire isn't hiding.

We whirl around at the click of a shotgun and find ourselves facing a middle-aged man with a long grey beard. The gun is shaking in his trembling hands. He appears to be in shock, and squints to recognize us. Or at least, one of us.

I observe this man through the flickering light of the campfire. He looks familiar. Suddenly, I realize who this is.

*Oh my god!*

# Chapter 8

# THE HILLS HAVE EYES

"D-DROP THE weapon," the man hisses through chattering teeth. He is shaking uncontrollably. This is not the man I am guessing he once was.

Mom slowly places her handgun on the grass.

"W-who are you? What are y-you d-doing here?"

"We're just passing through," Mom replies. "We don't mean you any harm."

"Just p-passing through? No one j-just passes through h-here. No one."

*Beth did.*

He presses his gun against Mom's chest.

"Tell m-me the truth. Who are you? What d-do you want with me?"

"Roy." I speak calmly. "Your name is Roy, isn't it?"

The man's nervousness transitions to shock. "How…how c-could you p-possibly know that?"

"I saw you in a photograph, posing with your wife Rose and your son Flint."

Roy is speechless.

"Flint and Rose are friends of mine. Now, can you please lower your gun?"

* * *

The four of us are sitting around the fire. Roy stokes the fire and for a brief moment of silence we all watch the flames grow. Shadows are dancing on the walls of his tent. Through the open flap I see a sleeping bag, clothing, and a pile of paperbacks.

"How…how are they?" Roy asks me. "Flint and Rose."

"They're good." There's no point telling him about the hell Cole put them through. "Rose said you left for a supply run and never came back. They think you're dead."

"It's better that way."

"How could it be better for them without you? Don't you think Flint should have a father in his life?"

"I've done things. Unthinkable things. I tried to justify them by telling myself it was all for my family. Deep down I knew I was wrong. My actions were unforgivable. I could barely look Rose in the eye."

We give Roy a minute to revisit his undesirable memories and process them, as he has probably done countless times around this fire. Beth tosses another log on, even though it isn't needed. Mom crosses her arms and closes her eyes. I just sit and listen to the crackling flames.

"I never went on that supply run," Roy continues quietly. "I walked into the fog and didn't stop. Expected there to be nothing but trees and mist, and figured I would eventually starve to death. That would have been okay.

Instead, this place became my new home. A valley where there was no one for me to hurt. The monster that lives down there is perfect company for a monster like me."

Beth shakes her head.

I don't ask what Roy's crimes were, but have my suspicions. "I lost my father not long ago. He did unspeakable things too." I glance at my mom. "So did my mom."

"Syn…"

"But when I lost my dad I realized that no matter what my parents did, and no matter what crimes they committed, I couldn't stop loving them. I still wanted them in my life. I'd do anything to have my dad back."

Mom places a hand on my shoulder.

"A boy deserves to be with his father," I go on. "No matter what you might have done, Flint needs you in his life. Rose should know that you're alive."

Roy is silent, burdened with shame. "Don't tell them. I need to atone, alone. They are better off without me."

He leaves us for a moment and returns with a bucket of water to douse the fire. "Stay here for the night. I'll show you the way to the Garden tomorrow."

"I know how to get there," Beth says.

"The shortcut, I'm guessing? It never stays in one place." Roy is staring at Beth.

"What?" she asks.

"I remember you. You were the little girl in the Garden, and you came to the valley. I saw you from up here. The monster was chasing you."

"Really? Thanks for the assist."

Roy looks ashamed.

"The monster doesn't come up here?" I ask.

"It can't balance on the incline. I set traps just in case it tries."

"What kind of traps?"

"The kind that go boom?" Beth asks.

"Exactly. You're lucky you didn't set off any while climbing up here."

We have been dodging arrows ever since we were attacked in my bedroom. When Aunt Ruth…

Roy hands each of us a blanket and we lay them side by side on the grass.

The night air is warm and fresh, aside from the occasional cloud of smoke from the dying fire. I lie back and gaze at the stars, my nerves calmed by the sound of the waterfall. I think of Aunt Ruth, of her final moment.

Beth gently takes my hand, as if she can read my mind.

* * *

The ground is shaking. I jump to my feet. "Mom! Beth!"

It's morning. The sound of thundering footsteps is loud enough to be heard over the waterfall.

BOOM, BOOM, BOOM!

I leap backwards in terror at the monstrous call that echoes throughout the valley, part wail, part roar.

Roy startles me further, suddenly appearing beside me. "The beast has risen."

# Chapter 9

# THE MARK OF THE BEAST

EVEN THOUGH A MONSTER RAMPAGES below, this is the most beautiful place I have ever seen. The valley is about the size of the Garden, but instead of firs, pines, and shrubs, there are palm trees and other trees growing delectable, ripe fruit. Small creatures scamper about: bunnies, squirrels, and birds.

The waterfall looks like a postcard scene, careening over the side of the hill into a lagoon of glistening blue water. A wall of fog borders the valley, just like in the neighboring Garden. The air is humid, yet with the partial healing properties, I have no problems breathing.

"This is Masie's test site," Mom says.

"It's beautiful."

"If it wasn't for the beast, your father and I would have set up shop here."

"That thing is on you."

"It is. Our first failed attempt to bring life to the Garden."

"Life such as reptiles, rodents, birds and even children's pets?"

"Yes."

"And people?"

Mom nods solemnly. "That thing is an atrocity," she admits, pausing as more thundering footsteps shake the ground.

"Yeah, it thrives by eating its young."

"It's the circle of life, Syn."

I laugh, sarcastically. "No, Mom. That really isn't the circle of life."

I turn away. Roy and Beth are huddled outside his tent, engrossed in conversation. They become silent when they see me approaching.

"What are you talking about?"

"Nothing," Beth says.

Roy is avoiding eye contact with me.

"I don't believe you."

Roy deflects my scrutiny with an offer of breakfast and though I am determined to know what they're up to, hunger supersedes my suspicions.

The fruit he serves us is juicier and tastier than any I have ever eaten. Oranges, bananas, grapefruit, mangos. Mom and Beth opt for grapefruits and I savor a banana. Eating grapefruit causes a harmful interaction with some of my meds. Despite the partial healing properties here, I still have medication in my system and don't want to take any chances.

The ground shakes again, followed by a bloodcurdling shriek. The monster is having breakfast too.

That thought makes my skin crawl and I lose my appetite.

Roy stands up and I follow him to the cliff, leaving Mom and Beth out of earshot.

"It was you, wasn't it?" I ask. "You killed those people in the Garden."

"I did."

Just as I had guessed. Everyone in the Garden assumed Cole killed the people who started the war between humans and Creepers. But Cole was just a boy. He wouldn't have had the strength to drag people to the top of the stairway and heave them off the platform. Cole used the murders to convince the humans that the Creepers were responsible and had to be stopped. So, it was Roy who killed those people. That was his sin. Cole simply used the resulting fear to his advantage.

Roy discretely lifts the bottom of his shirt to reveal reptilian scales on his back.

*Just like Flint.*

"Some humans were becoming hostile towards the Creepers before they were banished underground. A few figured out that Flint was a Creeper, or at least the son of a Creeper. Someone threatened my family. After I...did what I did...some suspected me of the crime. They were right of course, and I feared for my family if word got out.

"I didn't foresee the toll the guilt would take on me. What kind of person murders people in cold blood like that? What kind of father could I be? I was afraid to leave a mark on my son. Afraid that he would grow up and become just like his monstrous father."

"Flint is a good kid."

"I'm glad to hear that."

"Would you consider coming back to the Garden with us?"

"No. And don't tell them I am alive. Promise me."

"Okay." This is a promise I'm not sure I can keep.

"What are you guys talking about?" Beth asks, sneaking up from behind with Mom.

"Nothing."

"Touché." She smirks.

"Girls, I found our way out," Mom says. She points to what certainly looks like a voltway in the distance. The electrical currents encircling the black abyss are as clear as if they were eight feet in front of us.

"That's about a twenty-minute walk," Roy says. "You'll have to travel through the beast's prime territory."

Beth rolls her eyes. "Of course we will."

"No, we won't," Mom says. "We'll enter the fog and walk around the perimeter of the valley. Avoid the creature completely."

"I wouldn't advise that," Roy says. "We can barely see a few feet in front of us in the fog, while the beast has no problem seeing in the dark. At least in the valley we can see it and where we are going. In the fog, we're easy pickings."

"Great," Beth says.

"I'll guide you. Just stay as quiet as possible and we should be fine. I have made it this long, after all."

We gather our things and descend the hill, carefully following Roy to avoid any of his traps. We make it to the bottom without blowing up.

*So far, so good.*

"I think it might be sleeping again," whispers Beth.

As if on cue, the ground rumbles, twenty times worse than it did atop the hill. We can barely hold our footing.

I stagger into Beth, almost knocking her over. "Nice jinx."

"Shhh." Roy holds a nervous finger up to his lips.

My eyes drift to the ground to balance my footing and I gasp. I am standing in the belly of one colossal footprint. The mark of the beast.

# Chapter 10

# AS I WALK THROUGH THE VALLEY OF THE SHADOW OF DEATH

THE FOOTPRINT IS HALF THE size of an SUV. It appears that the monster has three toes and a pointed heel that gouges into the ground. To my left is the matching footprint. I look up and follow everyone's gaze. The path marking the monster's romp is going in the same direction we are headed.

"If we make contact, whatever you do, don't look at it."

Mom's whisper is so faint, I can barely make out her warning.

"Just run," she adds earnestly.

"Why can't we—"

"Your mother is right," Roy whispers, quickly glancing at Beth. "Don't look at it."

"But why not?"

"Shhh!" Roy hisses. "Stay quiet."

*Will we be turned to stone, like when looking into Medusa's eyes? Or will our faces melt off like in Raiders of the Lost Ark?*

"Let's get moving," Roy orders.

We quickly make our way through the western part of the valley, pushing through lush, emerald-green tropical plants. The waterfall sounds louder with every passing minute. I catch a glimpse of a rabbit, a mouse and a vole, and a snake slithers under a rock. These are undoubtedly some of the creatures that make up the DNA of the monster—its offspring and lunch specials.

As the mist from the waterfall moistens my cheeks, the ground rumbles and the monster's screech echoes throughout the valley for a long, agonizing moment. Once again, it's on the move. And once again, we have to stop.

A pile of rocks is blocking our path. Roy beckons to me and Beth. He hoists us up one at a time to the top of the first mammoth-sized boulder. I struggle to hold my footing on the jagged, slippery surface. He helps Mom climb up and though it's a struggle, pulls himself up too.

It's a precarious climb to the top of the pile of boulders. More screeching from the monster is unnerving and it's hard to concentrate on keeping my balance, especially when the horrific sound makes my heart pound and I want to run for my life. After about a half hour though, we finally reach the top and stop to catch our breath.

Roy is pensive. "The path is blocked by that stone wall. We'll have to use this rocky ledge. Be very careful."

The surface narrows as we follow the sound of the waterfall. Finally, the waterfall I have only listened to until now comes into view. Having never traveled too far from home (alternate worlds aside), I can honestly say this is one of the most beautiful settings I have seen. A rush of water cascade down into a tranquil turquoise pool. I try to make out where the water is coming from but it's too high up.

"It's beautiful," says Beth.

The ground rumbles again. Right, we're not in an exotic paradise, we're evading a monster that would have made a T. Rex quiver in its metaphorical boots.

If we walk straight ahead we will fall into the lagoon. Roy motions to us that we should follow the narrow rock ledge that borders the lagoon.

The warm mist from the falls feels heavenly. The rumbling earth from monstrous footsteps, not so much.

Beth screams when I lose my footing and fall into her, pushing us both too close to the edge. Roy reaches for my arm and misses, and we both tumble into the water. Mom jumps in after us and holds my head above water. Beth manages just fine, as usual. Roy dives in as the thundering and screeching grows louder.

BOOM, BOOM, BOOM!

The mist from the falls is thicker down here and my lungs are aggravated by it despite the healing properties. The stress certainly doesn't help either. I stifle a cough. The booming abruptly stops. Mom and Roy are hovering over us in the water. All is silent, except for the roar of the falls.

The monster wails again, so close and so piercing, I fear my eardrums will explode. Despite the churning sound of water, I can hear the monster's heavy breathing. It's sniffing out its prey.

Us!

The monster's shadow is looming over us. I recall what Mom said. *Don't look at it.* I lower my eyes, though her warning tempts me to want to peek.

BOOM, BOOM, BOOM!

The monster has stormed off. Maybe the water is masking our scent. Who cares? We're alive.

A minute passes. Mom looks at Roy quizzically and he nods. They help us back onto the ledge.

"What next, Mom?" Beth asks. "I think we need to—"

BOOM, BOOM, BOOM!

Its footsteps are more rapid. It's running this way!

Roy motions us forward. "Move out!"

Balancing on the ledge, we move as quickly as possible. It's slippery now that we're dripping wet, but we make it past the lagoon safely and climb onto a larger stone platform. From there, the voltway is within sight! A twenty-second run from here, while weighted down by drenched clothing!

BOOM, BOOM, BOOM!

Mom and Roy climb down to the gardens a few feet below and raise their arms to guide us down.

"Follow me!" Roy yells, no longer bothering to whisper.

We run through brush, stumbling as the ground shakes. We're so close, but so is the monster.

*We're not going to make it!*

Roy sprints ahead, waving his arms in the air. "Hey, you ugly brute! Over here!"

*What is he doing?*

"Please don't tell Rose or Flint that you saw me!"

Then to our horror, Roy runs in the direction of the monster. Movement from the corner of my eye distracts me to a sight that brings utter terror—a dark green scaly tail with jagged white spikes. This tail is large enough to be a monster all on its own. It lumbers past where Roy had just been.

"Run!" Mom orders.

As I'm gasping my last breath of paradise's fresh air, I hope that Roy is luring the monster away and not sacrificing himself.

I leap into the voltway and once again am in the pitch-black Oblivion. There is no light and no sound. Nothing. Until a familiar image resurfaces: Me, with Aunt Ruth, in the Garden.

*I lean close to tell her something. She looks terribly concerned.*

This isn't a projection of something to come. The woman I knew as Aunt Ruth is gone, so that is impossible. However, with all the events I saw the first time I entered the Oblivion, this is the only one I see now. What makes this event more significant than the others?

Then just like that, I am no longer in the pitch-black abyss. I am with Mom and Beth in the sewers beneath the Garden.

*We made it!*

# Chapter 11

# THE MESSENGER

I TUNE IN TO THE familiar sound of dripping water echoing off the dank sewer walls, which are still lit by battery-powered lights. It's darker than usual. The batteries have to be replaced in some of the lights.

The excess mucus in my lungs has practically cleared up. I'm not happy about being back in the Garden, but the silver lining is feeling like a healthy teenager again. A silver lining so many in my position would accept without a second thought.

Beth is already exploring our surroundings. That girl is always on the ready. There is no one in sight, for now.

As we walk through the sewers looking for humans or Creepers, my thoughts return to Roy. I hope he is okay. He risked his life for strangers. Perhaps an attempt to atone for his past, to prove to himself that he doesn't have to be a monster. At least not anymore.

The last two times I was in this location, I heard the rumbling of hundreds of rats that were scurrying around. We're right outside the room where the rats were bred to feed the poor souls who were forced to live in these murky tunnels. I peer through the window. It's dark. And very quiet. Likely no rats.

Beth had told me that the humans and Creepers were living in relative peace, so there would be no reason for anyone to live in this depressing place anymore.

"It's unlikely we'll find anyone here." Beth's voice echoes through the tunnel.

They've moved on and are waiting for me to catch up. I take a moment to wring as much water from my hair as possible from our unexpected swim in the valley.

"Come on, Syn." Mom gestures impatiently. She's waiting under the sewer grate that exits to the Garden.

Once we're in the fog, I see lightways flashing in the distance, just like the first time I was here. When I returned to rescue Beth, lightways were appearing in the Garden instead. Along with the healing properties, Mom has restored the Garden to the way it was meant to be.

We exit the fog sooner than expected and when my eyes adjust to the sunlight, it's clear that things have changed.

The fog has receded and the living area has expanded. A forest is growing in the common area. The border of fog is now within the woods. More cabins have been built, doubling the capacity of living quarters.

"The humans and Creepers cut down trees within the fog," says Beth. "They built new homes to accommodate everyone."

"I like what this place has become."

"It's because of you both," says Mom. "If you girls hadn't rallied the humans and Creepers to fight Cole, this place would still be in disarray."

That may very well be true, but it was my brash actions that led to humans being trapped in the sewers in the first place, not to mention my destroying the Garden's healing properties. That's something I've had a hard time forgiving myself for, and surely some of the people here feel the same way.

The Garden is once again meticulously landscaped. Flowers that wouldn't be in season at this time of year at home are blooming in lush beds. The grass is a deep verdant green, and evenly groomed. A beautiful wooden bridge has been built across the pond.

"There's Nell!"

Lily's best friend is leaning on the wooden railing and Nell looks up when she hears my voice. She waves and smiles, though there is brief hesitation.

"Don't worry," Beth says. "it'll be fine."

"You're right," I lie, and wave back.

"Attagirl!"

Startled by the new voice from behind us, I whirl around. There is nobody there.

"Look!" says Beth.

Right before our eyes, the faint outline of a woman is forming in mid-air.

*Now what?*

Mom raises her gun.

There is laughter and the form jovially says, "Oh dear Syn. You've been away far too long."

We recognize the voice, and Beth lowers her weapon.

I'm relieved as our friend Crystal (chameleon ability, not shy) appears in front of us, wearing nothing but her birthday suit.

When we first met we were enemies, until Crystal eventually stood up for me and Beth. That almost got her killed.

"I'm so glad you're back," says Crystal.

"In the flesh." Beth grins.

"I don't suppose you want to put something on?" I tease.

"That makes it harder to sneak up on people." She winks. "Will you guys be staying awhile?"

Mom glances at the house. "Indefinitely."

"Glad to hear it." Crystal doesn't pick up on Mom's lack of enthusiasm.

"Girls, I'm going to the house to make sure the Garden is secure."

"Okay, Mom. Beth and I will visit Rose and Flint."

Crystal claps her hands excitedly. "Oh, they'll be thrilled to see you!"

"We'll see." I lack her optimism.

Rose's cabin is in sight when we see Mitchell (Turtle-Man), another enemy-turned-friend. His appearance has changed drastically. He used to have a turtle shell attached to his back, where he could pull his appendages inside to shelter himself.

"Mitchell!" I call to this portly man who no longer resembles a Creeper. "I know that Cole tore the shell off your back, but I assumed that it grew back when the Garden's healing properties were restored."

"I shave the new growth every couple of days. It's itchy, but I feel like a new man. Like a big weight has been lifted off my shoulders."

*Literally.*

Beth playfully pokes his chest. "And you're harder to tip over now."

"Exactly. Welcome back, girls. It's a beautiful day!"

Mitchell is so much happier now. Maybe I did do some good here after all. When we arrive at Rose's cabin, I knock on the door apprehensively. Flint helped me when I was in trouble last time, so I think he'll be happy to see me. I'm unsure about Rose though. They went through a lot after Cole took over the Garden.

There's no answer, so Beth peeks through a window. "Nobody home."

I feel relieved. "Okay, there is someone else I want to see before we meet Mom at the house."

A few minutes later, Beth knocks on Lily and Fawn's door. It creaks open a tad and she pushes it farther. The main living space is empty. There is giggling coming from the second room though. We stop just outside the room.

"Hello?" I call out, quietly.

"Nobody can hear you, Scaredy-cat." Impatiently, Beth pokes her head through the open doorway, with me peering over her shoulder.

Lily and Lundy are making out on the unkempt bed. Lily yelps when she sees us.

"What the—! Ever hear of knocking?" She's blushing.

"I'm sorry. The door was—"

"Whatever." She leaps off the bed and greets me. "I thought you weren't coming back!"

"I wasn't. We're kind of…"

"We're on the lam," Beth says.

"Why doesn't that surprise me? I hope that whatever gong show you're running from doesn't find its way here."

"No, it won't. That isn't possible."

"Good."

"It's good to see you, Syn." Lundy greets me with a sheepish grin.

"You too. So…you guys…is this new?"

"Not really." Lundy places one arm around Lily's shoulders. "We've been together for a while."

"I'm happy for you."

"Thanks, Syn." Lily kisses Lundy on the cheek.

"Lily, I might be in the Garden for a while. Are you and I going to be okay?"

"Yeah. I'm just surprised to see you."

"I'm surprised to be back."

"It's just…things have been really good here. Better than they have been in a long time. What happened wasn't really your fault, but just please—"

"It wasn't her fault at all," Beth says firmly. "Whoever we're running from can't get here. Okay?"

"Okay." Lily hugs me again. "It's really nice to see you. Both of you."

"Mom is waiting for us, Syn."

"We'll catch up with you two later, okay? I just wanted to say hello." I wave, feeling a little heat in my cheeks. "Sorry to interrupt."

Beth makes sure the front door is closed tightly after we leave. "Guess I should have let you take the lead after all."

"Yeah…."

"What's up?"

"There is one more place I want to go before we rejoin Mom."

"I know."

Dad is buried in a new graveyard in the open green space next to the house. There are twenty-four graves for all the humans and Creepers who died during the battle with Cole. There is a grave for my friend Wolf—such a spry old man he was—and for

Nell's dad, Hopper. Both men died after I inadvertently destroyed the Garden's healing properties.

Dad's plot is in the row closest to the orchard, partly shaded by the wooden grave marker. Flowers have been laid on the grass that has grown over his resting place. I pause to read the words carved on his grave marker.

**Ian Wade**
**Loving Father & Husband**
**He Deserved Better**

*He deserved better?*

That isn't true. Younger, alternate versions of me, his own daughter, are buried less than a minute's walk away. They were experimented on. Tortured by my parents in hopes of discovering a cure for me. *They* deserved better.

Still, he was my father. I can't help but love him and wish that he was by my side rather than rotting in the ground.

Beth kneels beside me. "Try to remember the good times you had."

"That's not easy. They were always working and leaving me with a sitter. And then they were gone."

"Yeah, but they were often here working on a cure for your illness."

"That left little time for me."

"There has to be something good to remember."

My earliest memories of my parents are of them sitting next to me during hospital visits and helping me with my treatments. I try to remember more and recall Dad reading me bedtime stories like ones by *Dr. Seuss* or my favorite, *The Gingerbread Man.*

"I remember him tucking me in and leaving the nightlight on in the hall."

"You know he loved you."

I have no doubt he loved me as much as anyone possibly could. Both of my parents did horrible things, only because of their love for me.

I kiss two fingers and place them on the grass. "I love you, Dad."

I throw my arms around Beth and we hold each other, until voices from inside the house remind us we have a further destination.

The front door is ajar. Mom has a room on the second floor and the rest of the house is mostly used for storage, and contains the equipment that enables the Garden's healing properties and other unique features.

On the far side of the main floor, which is a replica of our living room at home, Mom is sitting at a round oak table, facing us. Maya (spider, woman, frenemy) is hanging from the ceiling on a strand of web. Mom looks past her when we enter and Maya spins around.

"Synthia. Beth." She acknowledges our presence formally.

"Hi Maya." My heart is heavy with apprehension.

"You should not have returned. I told your mother and I will tell you. You are endangering us all by seeking refuge here."

"And I told you, Maya," Mom begins, "there is absolutely no way for them to get in."

Maya whips around to face Mom again. "There is always a way!" She turns back to us. "Leave us now. Your mother and I have much to discuss."

When Beth and I reach the back of the house we are surprised to see Rose. I attempt to greet her, but pause midstride. Worry is etched upon her face.

*Does she know about Roy?*

"You need to come with me." Rose steers clear of pleasantries.

We follow her past the pond. Humans and Creepers seem friendly for the most part, some waving. Rose remains silent.

Flint is in the Square, waiting to welcome us. He's noticeably taller than the last time I saw him. Much taller than Beth, who is around the same age.

"Hi Beth. Hi Syn." He wraps his arms around me. "I've missed you guys."

"I've missed you too. Is everything okay?"

"I don't know."

Rose gestures for us to keep moving and soon I see someone I'd normally be happy to see. But here and now, all I feel is dread at the sight of my best friend. If Ebby has followed us here, we have a big problem.

She runs up to me in a panic. "Syn! Your aunt, but not really your aunt. And not just her, lots of them!"

Her panic has my stomach in knots. "What did they do?"

"They took him."

"Who did they take?"

"Jon!" she blurts. "They took Jon."

# Chapter 12

# BEGGING FOR MERCY

"EBBY." I SPEAK as calmly as possible. "Tell me exactly what happened."

We gather around and wait for her to collect her words as tears stream down her face. Rose hands her a tissue and she sits down on the grass. "When you didn't respond to our texts, Jon and I got worried and went to your place to check on you."

Not surprising. I always try to respond to messages as quickly as possible because if I don't, friends worry that my health might have taken a turn for the worse.

"You weren't home so we came back to my place. Before we even got our coats off, the doorbell rang. It was your aunt. And then, there were two. Exact lookalikes. Plus another, and another, and another. They came inside my house like it was theirs...."

"What happened?" I try to hurry this up.

"They made us sit down in the kitchen. One of them told us that they had to get into the Garden. They asked me and Jon which one of us was closest to you. Before I could even open my mouth, Jon said he was. I think he was trying to protect me." She glances at Flint, then Rose.

"What else?" Beth chimes in, impatiently.

"One of your, um, aunts, told us they will keep Jon. That I was to come here and tell you and your Mom to let them into the Garden or…they'll kill him."

"How long?" Beth asks. "How long did they say we have?"

"Forty-eight hours. That isn't all. After that time has passed, if you haven't let them in they will kill one of my parents. They will kill my other parent the next day." She is sobbing. "They will continue killing people you care about until you let them into the Garden."

Way in the back of my mind, I assumed something like this would happen. Perhaps it was denial that kept the thought buried. Regret claims my heart. "We should have closed the lightway to prevent anyone from coming here."

"Now it's too late," says Rose, her tone tainted with animosity.

"Syn, you'll do what they say?" Ebby asks. "Your mom won't let them hurt Jon, right?"

Ebby has heard enough about my mom to know that she would sacrifice the entire planet to save her children.

"Of course not, Ebby," I reassure her through clenched teeth. "She won't let anything happen to Jon or the rest of your family. I promise."

*Please let this be a promise I can keep.*

* * *

"Syn, I know that Jon was your boyfriend, but under no circumstances can we let Masie Winters into the Garden." Mom is speaking from her seat at the round table, while Maya takes everything in.

"Are you even able to let them enter the lightway?" I ask.

"It has been a long time since I have done that, but yes. That doesn't mean I will. The risk is too high."

"None of the Masies who chased us had weapons, Mom." I plead. "They could have come prepared and killed us if they wanted to. Maybe the Masies just want to reside in the valley they created."

"The valley?"

Mom ignores Maya's question. "Synthia, you know better than that. The Masie who raised you gave her life so we could escape. She knew what they are up to and we both know it can't be good."

"Your mother is right," Maya says. "You know this."

"What I know is that a person doesn't give up on the people they love. I never gave up on Beth, and against all odds I helped her escape from Cole."

"Let's ask young Bethany what she thinks," Maya says. "Should we allow a hostile force inside the gates of our community?"

Beth doesn't answer.

"Just as I th—"

"Syn is right," Beth interrupts Maya. "I'd be buried outside with the others if my sister hadn't risked everything for me."

Maya drops from the ceiling onto her human-like legs and looms over me. "I assisted in that rescue mission. Your sister may be here today, but many are not."

"I have lost almost everything," Maya insists. "Four of my children and their father. And you lost your father. There is a cemetery in the Garden full of casualties that weren't there before your little rescue mission. Your sister may stand by your side. Thomas and my children cannot stand by my side. Many of this Garden's loved ones are gone forever. And you ungrateful children wish to risk more lives to save that of one friend? You have learned nothing!"

"Maya," Mom says steadily. "I'm with you. Now get the hell out of my daughter's face."

Maya's eyes pierce through me as she scampers past and out the back door, leaving it swinging open on its hinges.

"What about Luke?" Mom asks me. "He can surely protect his parents."

"He's in Haiti, volunteering with Habitat for Humanity."

"There's the police," she suggests. "It's their job to—"

"*Really*, Mom? These women have waited more than ten years to carry out their plan. You seriously think they will let the police get in their way?"

Mom says nothing. Beth also remains silent. She supports me as her sister, but knows the risk of letting the Masies in.

As do I.

"Mom, you are right. So is Maya. But I can't sit back and do nothing while Jon is murdered, and maybe Ebby's parents too. I can't and I won't."

We're all consumed by a long, lingering silence.

Finally, Beth joins my side. "Neither will I."

Mom watches the back door swing open on a breeze. "It's not even up to me. It's not up to Maya. We assembled a council after you left and have to vote on anything that affects the residents. And I am telling you now, I will vote against this. For your sake, I must. Even if you hate me for it. I'll be shocked if you receive even one vote in favor. The people here have been through too much."

"I'll convince them." I am determined. "I'll convince them that we can come up with a plan to let the Masies in and still protect everyone."

"You are not listening to me, Syn."

"I'll talk to them too," Beth insists.

Mom combs both hands through her hair, exasperated. "I'll gather the council."

Chapter 13

# NIGHT AT THE ROUND TABLE

IT'S DARK BY THE TIME all council members have gathered at the round table where Beth and I faced Maya's wrath. Maya is the last to arrive.

"This better not be about what we discussed earlier." Maya springs over the table and clings to the wall, frowning at Beth and me.

The council is split evenly between humans and Creepers. The humans include Mom, Rose, Fawn, Lundy, and Docson. The Creepers are represented by Maya, Crystal, Larry (Ant-Man), Katya (Firefly-Woman), and Hogan (Croc-Man), who at one time hunted me but like Crystal, came around when it mattered most.

Mom rises to address Maya and the council. "We each have the prerogative to gather the council. All I ask is that everyone hears what my daughters have to say."

"Your daughters," Maya snarls, "should not even be here. A majority vote is required to allow anyone not on the council to attend our meetings."

"I ask that council allow Syn and Beth to have a voice in this meeting." Mom surveys the room and raises her hand. "I vote in favor."

While Lundy is the only other human to raise his hand, all the Creepers, aside from Maya, vote in favor.

"You may stay," Mom tells us.

I thank the council.

"Why don't I summarize what the children would like to articulate?" Maya says, before I can get a word in. "Years ago, Debra and her husband barred an evil woman from the Garden: Masie Winters. Now, dozens or perhaps hundreds of this woman's others from different worlds have formed an army. In order to gain access to the Garden for what are surely nefarious purposes, they have threatened to kill the childrens' friend, among others, if Debra does not let them in."

The group bursts into concerned chatter.

"Did I leave anything out, child?" Maya taunts.

"You skipped over the fact that we'll be prepared for the worst," Beth snaps.

"My apologies," Maya says sarcastically. "I had forgotten. By sunrise, you will have a plan to defend us from this army of doom."

"We have weapons from the battle against Cole," I tell her.

"Against Cole and each other," Maya reminds us. "We did not exactly all fight side by side."

"That's in the past," I say. "So we arm ourselves, hide in the trees and bushes. If they attack, we fight back."

"Oh, Child," Maya teases, "that is most adorable. Your mighty plan is to *fight back*. I do remember a much more sophisticated, well-thought-out defense strategy that your friend Luke prepared. His plan of attack was detailed and formulated with footnotes for surprises that may arise. If my memory serves me right, he still ended up with a bullet in his belly. Were there not many other casualties? Despite this great strategy to attack, your very own father ended up impaled. He left quite a nasty blood stain on the forest floor.

Beth climbs onto the table and lunges at Maya. Maya shoots a strand of web at Beth's leg and she loses her footing. She lands hard on the table, on her back.

Hogan abruptly rises from his chair. "Maya, she's just a child."

"A child you were perfectly willing to kill less than a year ago," Maya reminds him.

"I was wrong."

Beth yanks Maya's web off her leg and hops down from the table, her eyes glued to Maya. "You mention my father again and I'll kill you."

"Maya, if you lay your web on either of my daughters again, *I* will kill you." Mom says. "That's a promise."

"Everyone, sit down!" Crystal yells. "There are children present. Let's act like adults."

The council members return to order and Mom sits down.

"Synthia," Rose says. "I realize you have been through a lot and I hate to think you will lose your friend. Nobody deserves that. Jon is a nice boy. My Flint is a nice boy too. As are the other children in the Garden. They don't deserve to die. None of us do. The fact that these women are threatening the life of a teenager to get what they want worries me. It should worry all of you too."

"But Rose—"

"Flint is my son. As a member of the council, everyone living here is my responsibility. I can't support this. I'm truly sorry, Synthia."

I don't fault her. How can I ask her to put her son's life at risk for someone else? She is a mother first.

Katya raises a hand. "Rose is right."

"Oh, don't you dare!" Beth shouts. "You were perfectly content to hand us over to a psychopath."

"Listen, Kid." Katya says, "You played the guilt card already, remember? We have all wronged many. The Creepers and humans wronged each other, but we have moved past that."

"We had to," Docson says. "We are in a good place now."

"I'm a mother too," Fawn explains. "I can't put Lily's life at risk."

"Syn," Lundy says, "I wish I could help you. Jon is a good guy."

"I support Syn and Beth," Larry proclaims. "We owe it to them."

"I'm with Larry," Crystal asserts. "We'll arm ourselves. We have guns, explosives, and the flame-thrower. Once Jon is safely returned, we blow the enemy to hell."

"With the Garden's healing properties, they won't die," Larry admits. "But you know what? Neither will we."

"An instant kill is permanent," Katya argues. "They break our necks or shoot a bullet into our brain and there is no coming back from that. Count me out."

"Count me in," Hogan says.

*Well,* **that** *is a surprise.*

Maya sneers at Hogan. "That is very noble of you to raise your hand when your position is clearly not going to reach a majority vote."

"Hold on a second!" Ebby strides into the room.

*So much for waiting upstairs.*

Katya springs from her chair. "Who is this? You're not authorized to be here."

"I am the girl you took hostage. Remember? You used me as a shield, with no concern that I might be killed. And now these maniacs have threatened to kill a member of my family for every day past Jon's execution that they are refused entry."

"We are not without sympathy." Maya speaks with great sincerity. "However, you must see our need to protect our own."

"How dare you!" Ebby raises her fists and storms at Maya.

I hold her back. "You don't want to do that."

"That is the first wise thing you have said since you returned, child." She eyes the group around the table. "Shall we carry on with an official vote?"

Mom shrugs. She knew the meeting would go like this.

I raise a hand. "May I address the council before the vote?"

"That only seems fair," Larry says.

Lundy raises a hand too.

"Alright, Synthia," Mom says.

"Ebby, wait for me outside."

"No way, Syn."

"Ebby." Beth takes her hand. "I'll go with you."

Once the back door has clicked shut, I begin. "I understand why you feel the way you do. Letting these monsters into the Garden is a stupid idea. We would be putting the life of every human and Creeper in danger by laying out the welcome mat."

Maya and Mom eye me suspiciously.

"However, while it would be stupid," I say, "it would also be right. These women are determined. They will find a way in eventually. By letting them in now, we save people's lives."

"Syn, you know very well that they've been trying to find a way in since your father and I locked them out over a decade ago. Their entire plan was to wait all these years for me or your father to come home, and then force us to allow them in."

"Thanks for the support, Mother." My words are drenched with sarcasm. "Yes, that is true. But do you actually think they will stop with Jon and Ebby's family? If they can't persuade you to let them in they will go after Lundy's family."

"Whoa," Lundy says. "That's going too far. No one even knows I'm here."

"Your family knows. Beth told me they visit often. Like my mom said, my property has been watched by the army of Masies for more than ten years. Trust me, they will send someone you know through to give you the same warning Ebby gave us."

"Incorrect," Maya blurts. "Your mother closed the lightway on your property this afternoon."

"Is that true?"

"If I hadn't left it open in the first place, we could have prevented them from using Jon against us."

I'm grasping at straws here.

"It's time to vote," Maya says.

"No," I plead. "This isn't about revenge."

Mom crosses her arms. "The Masies are lying."

"What if you're wrong? I believe we can save Jon, and Ebby and Luke's parents, and everything will be okay."

Mom is thoughtful.

"What could they possibly want other than revenge?" Katya asks.

"This place came to fruition because of Masie's scientific discoveries, which my parents stole. Maybe they just want to see the end result."

"That is enough!" Maya hops back onto the table. "We will vote now. All in favor of allowing this enemy into our home raise your hand."

Docson quickly raises his hand, and Larry, Crystal, and Hogan slowly follow suit. Maya was right. They knew they could appease me, without the vote passing. They give Katya a dirty look for not doing the same.

"I won't endanger us all. I won't do it," Katya says.

Lundy raises his hand.

"Lundy…?" Maya is stunned.

"Syn is right," he says. "They will eventually go after my family. I just…" He glances at me. "I know my vote will only bring us to a tie, but it gives me a clear conscience. I have to put my family first and support Syn and Beth."

"Thank you," I say.

"Stupid boy," Maya mumbles.

Mom is still deep in thought. She would never risk the lives of her children for anything.

"Alright," Maya says.

Lundy, Docson and the three Creepers lower their hands.

"All against?"

"Wait!" Mom uncrosses her arms and sits up in her chair.

"What now?!" Maya shrieks.

The room grows so quiet I could hear a pin drop. Mom raises her hand as high as she can and looks straight at Maya. "I vote in favor."

# Chapter 14

# THREAT ASSESSMENT

MAYA IS LIVID. "Traitors!" She springs from the wall to the center of the table, casting her eyes at each offender as she speaks. "You are going to get us all killed!"

Nerves have been rattled by Maya's accusation. Especially for those who voted to support me. Docson is confident with his vote, but Lundy's feelings of doubt are obvious. I'm certain the Creepers only voted in favor because they thought no one else would. No one expected my Mom to suddenly change her mind.

*Why **did** Mom change her mind?*

Maya webs one of Mom's hands to the table and leans so close their faces are practically touching. "You have your children's best interests at heart and that is the commonality we share. But this reckless decision of yours puts all of our children at risk."

Mom shows no fear.

"What are you not telling us, Debra?"

"I just want to do the right thing."

The corners of Maya's mouth curl into a sinister grin. "To do the right thing? I know you better than that, Debra Wade. Even your own children know you better than that."

*She's not wrong.*

"You are making a grave mistake, Debra. I will make a promise to every traitor in this room right now. If anything happens to my Jeremy, I swear in the names of my fallen children and husband that I will rip out your throats and suck every ounce of blood from your useless bodies."

Maya spins a web over the glowing machine that powers the Garden's healing properties and swings out of sight. The Creepers and Lundy file outside through the front door, clearly downtrodden.

"Thanks, Lundy," I call after him, hopeful. He doesn't look back.

"I guess this meeting is over," says Mom. She tries to free herself from Maya's webbing.

Beth re-enters with Ebby and raises her eyebrows when she sees Mom stuck to the table.

"Wait!" Ebby says. "Don't tell me…. No, tell me! Syn?"

"Majority in favor!"

Ebby squeezes me so hard my feet lift off the ground. Beth skips over to Mom and high-fives her free hand.

"Okay, girls. Does someone want to give me a hand?"

I sit down next to Mom after all the excitement has subsided. "Thank you."

"Of course, Synthia. You know I would do anything for you."

*That is exactly what I am afraid of.*

# Chapter 15

# SKYFALL

THE SUN WARMS MY SKIN and a light breeze tousles my hair. My appreciation for the spring-like weather in winter only distracts me for a moment as the residents of the Garden cross my path. A few wave or say hi, though most avoid eye contact. I am guessing that many of the Creepers are remorseful of their actions towards Beth. The humans, on the other hand, associate my presence with trouble and realize that my being in the Garden again and the call for a gathering is unlikely a coincidence.

The members of the council, except for Maya, form a line in front of the spiral staircase. I'm at the back of the pack of Garden residents. Beth has chosen to be front and center.

Mom does most of the talking. She dives right into the necessary details about the small army of Masies who are demanding entry into the Garden, the kidnapping of Jon, and the decision of the council to allow the Masies entry in exchange for his freedom.

I am not at all surprised they don't take it well. Shouting escalates to a deafening roar of indiscernible words. I push through the unruly crowd towards Mom while she tries to quiet everyone down.

Suddenly, a scream pierces through the shouting and a young woman falls from the sky into the crowd, crashing onto Lobster-Man. The crowd gasps as some folk barely scramble to safety. The young woman is about my age and is impaled on one of Lobster-Man's claws. All is deathly quiet, except for Lobster-Man moaning.

Great. People are still falling from the sky, from a world Beth and I visited where masked cultists throw innocent people into a crater—a crater that was the aftermath of Mom and Dad ripping out the very earth to create the Garden. We learned this when visiting Doom World, and falling through the crater ourselves! After falling through the Oblivion, a lightway dropped us through to the sky over the Garden. We nearly didn't survive to tell the tale.

"My legs are broken," Lobster-Man groans. He starts to pry the girl from his bloody claw, wincing.

*Ugh.*

"I think my arm is broken too."

"You're lucky to be alive," says Beth.

He is. The Garden's healing properties are already taking effect. He will be as good as new in no time.

Lobster-Man quickly frees himself from the girl, leaving a hole where her heart used to be. I have to look away.

Two more bodies crash to the ground behind the crowd, both dead on impact. The crowd is humming with questions and accusations.

"This has been happening more often," Greeta says, her tentacles slowly waving around her face.

What craziness is occurring in Doom World? Hopefully, I will never find out.

Crystal climbs to the sixth step of the spiral staircase. "Quiet!" When the noise settles down, she continues. "I'll keep watch for more fallers. Meanwhile, don't all yell at once. No one can hear you. Now, Debra has something to say."

"Thank you, Crystal." Mom faces the crowd. "The council has decided, so there is no debate to be had. It is a done deal. Now we must plan how to protect ourselves in case things go badly."

The overwhelming crowd rage returns and once again, nothing anyone says can be heard.

"Hey!" Hogan's voice is lost in the din. He joins Crystal on the staircase. "Shut up! Everyone, just shut up!"

The cacophony of voices halts.

"We came to this decision because this is a friend of the two girls many of us have wronged. Not that the council needs to justify its decision. This is happening, like it or not. So you can either natter about it or we can prepare ourselves for the worst-case scenario."

Mumbling erupts from the crowd again, but for the most part people are listening. An hour later, several details have been decided and Mom recaps a few important ones.

"Hogan will plan our defense."

He nods at me, smiling.

"Anyone is free to take refuge in other worlds," she continues, "if they fear what is to come. The Garden residents who decide to stay will split into groups to either gather weapons or join Hogan for strategic defense planning."

I shuffle through the crowd to Mom's side and wave my arms. "Wait a minute everyone. I want to say something."

A hush descends.

"When this is all over, I will leave the Garden forever. That is a promise."

"Where have we heard that before?" Clover sneers. "We won't get our hopes up."

The remainder of the crowd breaks up amidst awkward laughter. Beth, Mom, Lundy, Ebby, and I stay behind.

"Girls, I am going to reeducate myself with the security program that keeps Masie out of the Garden. It's been a while and it's important to make sure I can let them in when the time comes." Mom heads to the house, satisfied that everything is in order.

"Lily is making lunch for us," says Lundy, "and since I'm starved. I'll race ya!"

"You're on!" Beth darts after him.

"You guys go ahead. I want to chat with Ebby."

"Thanks for everything," Ebby says.

"It's going to be okay. Jon and your family will be fine."

"Do you actually believe that?"

I gently hold her by the shoulders. "Everything will be okay. You'll see."

Aunt Ruth gave her life so that the Masies would never receive access to the Garden. I have grave concerns that everything will be *far* from okay.

# Chapter 16

# WINTERS IS COMING

THE FOLLOWING MORNING, AROUND thirty humans and Creepers are gathered on the lawn in front of the house. All eyes are on the porch as if it was a podium and a highly anticipated speaker is about to step up to the microphone.

Some of us are visibly armed. Mom and Beth are concealing their weapons. Most of the Garden residents are hiding behind bushes or in trees. They are armed to some degree, whether with guns, smoke bombs, or wooden bats—just some of the countless weapons that had been stored after last year's battle.

Mom and the most threatening Creepers are positioned at the front: Hogan, Greeta, Rat-Girl, and the always jaw-dropping Snake-Man (a literal jaw-dropper with a friggin' rattlesnake for a tail). The Creeper dogs sit with the front line, panting tongues hanging to the ground from their crock-like snouts, scaly skin glistening in the sunlight. The Creeper birds are perched on the roof, ready for a taste of the enemy if worse comes to worst.

Lundy is hiding in the fog behind us with the flame-thrower. Everyone is waiting in the Garden, prepared for a fight, except for those with young kids. They are hiding in the safety of their homes or down in the sewers. Maya hasn't been seen since the council meeting.

Beth, Ebby, and I are standing in the middle of the crowd. We're close enough to see what's happening, but far back enough so we can run if necessary.

Ebby is ready to go home. She can't be faulted for that. If I could leave, I would. Perhaps everything will be okay and once the Masies arrive that will be an option.

*Wishful thinking.*

Mom raises her computer tablet. "Everyone ready?"

The crowd responds with plenty of grumbling and she raises her voice. "I asked if you are ready, not if you are happy about it." She taps the tablet and a lightway appears thirty feet in front of her.

We wait.

Thirty minutes pass, then an hour. My stomach is growling and I'm not the only one who's hungry. Lily, Nell, and Mitchell hand out sandwiches. Peanut butter and banana, and tuna with celery. Larry and Fawn are on paper plate duty, and Rat-Girl and Butterfly Man pass out water bottles that are surely "borrowed" from some other world.

Mom orders us to eat at alternate times so we aren't all caught off guard when our visitors arrive.

Another hour passes. Our backs and legs would be stiff if it weren't for the Garden's healing properties. The properties don't help with fatigue and boredom though. Chatter erupts.

Some think they may not be coming. That all our concerns and preparations have been for nothing.

Obviously, the Masies were expecting the lightway to appear. It's been placed prominently in front of our house. Beth and I deduce that we're being made to wait so that when they arrive we are tired and caught off guard. Or perhaps they're showing us that they are the ones calling the shots.

Enough time passes that many are getting hungry again. We didn't plan for this to take so long. No one thought we'd have to provide dinner.

"Mom, what if people take turns going home and having a bite?"

"What do you think happens if our guests arrive and attack while half of us are gone?" Mom says. "Our entire defense plan would be useless."

"Nobody is coming," says one man.

"We're wasting our time," says another.

Mom and Hogan try to keep everyone calm but the crowd has grown restless.

"We've been here for more than four hours!"

Most are ready to leave. Voices are raised when Masie Winters—one of them anyway—casually exits the lightway as though she is stepping off an elevator.

"Get back into position!" Mom orders.

Another Masie follows. And another. Eight identical women have arranged themselves in a horizontal line in front of us.

The Masies inhale the fresh air with such satisfaction it would seem that Redfern's air quality is akin to Mumbai's. Eventually, two dozen Masies are stationed before us, each wearing a slightly different outfit.

Nobody speaks. Even Ebby, who I know is wondering the same thing I am.

*Where is Jon?*

Had they never intended to bring Jon? Maybe they've already done something terrible to him.

There are at least three dozen triumphant Masies lined up by the time Jon finally hobbles from the lightway.

"Jon!" Ebby moves forward, but I pull her back.

Jon is trembling. One Masie passes Jon to another Masie. He is passed from Masie to Masie, until hidden from our view.

"We need to get him!" Ebby is desperate.

"We will," I assure her. "I promise."

Another Masie comes through the lightway. There is seemingly no end, as one by one their army grows.

# Chapter 17

# WINTERS IS HERE

MOM, ALONG WITH THE others in the front row, is within arm's length of the enemy. The final Masie Winters bows her head to the others. I attempt a count of the intruders and get thirty-six. Beth counts forty-two. Little smarty-pants is probably dead on.

Each Masie takes in the surroundings with awe. The one nearest to Mom pulls a razor blade from her pocket and slashes one of her palms. The razor blade is passed to every Masie. Each watches with astonishment as the bleeding slows and the cut begins to heal right before her eyes.

"Spectacular," says Razor-Blade Masie. "Debra, you do realize the breakthrough you and Ian have achieved?"

"Debra, will Ian be joining us?" another Masie asks, sarcastically.

"The boy," Mom growls. "We let you in. Now hand over the boy."

"Of course," Razor-Blade Masie says. "First, we have a few errands to run."

Four Masies come forward and the group fills the void.

"Once these ladies have accomplished their tasks without incident," Razor-Blade Masie says, "we will hand over the boy."

Mom stares Masie down. "Fine."

Two of the four Masies go inside the house. The other two pass it by and are soon out of sight.

"You should know…that we are—"

"Armed," a voice from the back of the pack completes Mom's sentence.

The group makes way for this Masie to move to the front. She appears taller than the others, but only because of her stylish black boots with two-inch heels. Unlike the other women who are dressed in beige and navy blue, this Masie is wearing black jeans and a bright red blouse. Thick mascara adorns her long eyelashes, red lipstick shines on her lips, and her cheeks are defined by rosy pink blush.

"I assure you," Make-Up Masie addresses everyone, "that we are not here to hurt anyone. This Garden you're in only exists because Debra and Ian Wade stole our research. But we are here now, at last, and hold no ill will."

*Riiiight.*

"We only want to witness this marvelous creation our research has inspired."

"You threatened Jon and my family so you can go sightseeing?" Ebby shouts.

"Debra and Ian locked us out of this world. There was no other way."

Fed up with standing on the sidelines, I storm up to Make-Up Masie with Beth and Ebby right behind me. I am livid, waving my finger at her. "My aunt would not have given her life if you weren't a danger to my sister and me!"

Her lips curl into what seems like a genuine smile, but within that smile is a hint of something sinister.

"Hello, Syn." She waves. "Told you I would *see you soon.*"

# Chapter 18

# HOW I MET MY MURDERER

*HELLO SYN*
*SEE YOU SOON*

I will never forget the chills I felt in that other world after reading those words messily spray-painted in red. It was right after Beth and I had discovered the still-warm bodies of duplicates of myself and our parents, murdered in the kitchen of their house—*our* house. When we realized the killer was still in the house, we hid outside under a Jeep. After the killer drove away, we saw the chilling message on the driveway.

*HELLO SYN*
*SEE YOU SOON*

She knew we were there and let us go, believing that one day we would come face to face. *That day is today.*

The chills are back, along with some goosebumps on my forearms and the back of my neck. The woman who murdered another version of me in cold blood is staring into the depths of my soul.

Mom squeezes my hand.

I can barely find my voice. "It was you."

"Yes."

"You killed my family!" Beth shouts. "You went to different worlds and murdered them, again and again!"

"I only killed the family you came across."

"So who killed the other families?" I ask.

She gestures to the army of Masies. "We all did."

*What the hell?*

"You murdered people… versions of me… children… for some sort of sick revenge?"

"No Syn," Mom says. "This goes way beyond revenge."

"Give us Jon. Now!" I demand.

"We'll release your friend when our others have completed their tasks."

"Fine!" Beth snaps. "Explain this to us."

"Beth, I presume?"

Beth stares at Make-Up Masie with daggers in her eyes.

"In all of our travels to other worlds, we have never met another Wade girl."

"In all of my travels to other worlds," Beth says, "I have never met anyone I wanted to kill more."

The army collectively chuckles.

"Tell us what this is all about," I interject, hoping that if Beth just listens, she might avoid doing something rash with that gun of hers.

"As you now understand," Make-Up Masie begins, "the woman you believed was your aunt was actually your parents' lab partner at the university. In fact, in all of our respective worlds, we were colleagues of your parents.

"What you don't know is that your *aunt*—let's call her Ruth for simplicity—had been in communication with another world's Masie Winters. That Masie informed Ruth about your parents' betrayal. Ruth was furious. She wanted revenge."

"So it *is* about revenge," Beth insists.

"Originally, it was. However, after Ruth began to care for young Synthia, her anger waned and her plans for revenge faded."

"It's called love," Mom says.

I'm surprised to hear Mom acknowledge that the woman who killed her sister loved me.

"Don't be snide, Debra. We all know the murderous things you have done for love."

*We do.*

"The Masie who Ruth was in contact with wanted revenge and wasn't satisfied with Ruth's acceptance of the betrayal. She went back to her world and killed an alternate Syn and her parents. That left her feeling hollow, so she traveled to new worlds using Ruth's portals and convinced us to do the same."

"And let me guess," I say. "None of you were satisfied with simply killing my family."

"It was only a handful of us at that point, but you're correct. As it has been recorded for centuries, revenge is not as fulfilling as one would hope."

"So they died for nothing," I say. "Lovely."

"And you thought they deserved it because they stole your science fair project?" Beth snipes.

Make-Up Masie's face falls like Beth had wounded her beneath her armor. "Science fair project? Is that truly what you believe? We had all been working on one of mankind's greatest discoveries. Not only did we prove there was a multiverse, Ruth made it possible to travel between worlds and teleport from one place to another within one world. In a way, she created entirely new worlds. Like God.

"We couldn't replicate that work. Ruth's notes were here in this very Garden where your parents had blocked her and any other Masie from entering."

"Why do I suppose you are not going to just take those notes and leave?" I ask.

"Because, of course we will do no such thing," says Make-Up Masie. "We don't need to replicate anything because everything Ruth had devised has been applied right here in this Garden by your parents."

"You said only a handful of you had killed versions of my family for revenge. But a lot more than five of my families have been killed. You killed one just recently."

"Not for revenge. The Masie who befriended Ruth conjured up a new plan that would give us back what is ours, plus a whole lot more. Something amazing that would make up for what had been taken from us for more than ten years—something that would allow us to achieve our true potential, and give back to each of our worlds in a far greater capacity than we were originally able to provide. Masies recruited from different ends of the multiverse went out and recruited more. The initiation to prove their loyalty, to prove they weren't soft like your aunt, was to slaughter the Wade family in each of their respective worlds."

"That's what you were doing before you wrote that spray-painted message."

"Smart girl."

My riled-up sister is about to say something and I shake my head. Ruffling feathers won't help us. These are crazed murderers and we must watch what we say and do until Jon is freed. Even if we are prepared to fight, there would surely be casualties and the boy in their custody would be one of them.

"I can guess the rest of your story," I say.

"Be my guest," Make-Up Masie says.

"At least one of you, perhaps more, had been scouting out my family's property, hoping my parents would figure out a way home...."

"Go on."

"They never did. You thought it was hopeless but continued to keep watch, just in case. And then one day you saw this two-faced teenage boy push me into the pond. He followed me into the water and we both disappeared. You all hoped this might result in me coming home with my parents, except that when I returned I was alone. You were back at square one. Without my parents, there was no way you were getting into the Garden."

"Until two nights ago," Mom adds. "As soon as I was back, your scout recruited the troops and attacked us at our home."

"We didn't attack," Make-Up Masie says.

"You used me and my sister as leverage to force my Mom to give you access to the Garden."

"Yes, Synthia. After you escaped, we captured your friend. Now, here we are."

"Yes, here we are," Beth grumbles. "Waiting for your people to do who knows what."

"How lucky that we had a good story to share to pass the time." Make-Up Masie laughs.

"Kiss my—!"

"Bethany!" Mom yells, cutting Beth off.

"Really, Mom? Beth's choice of words is the problem you're choosing to deal with right now?"

"Syn," Make-Up Masie says. "As long as no one on your side does anything rash there is no problem. Revenge is in the past. We have moved on to bigger, better, bolder things. We must be in this Garden to achieve those things.

"Soon we'll free your friend and get started on our project. You girls can braid each other's hair and gossip about boys, or do whatever young girls do. You do your thing, we will do ours."

This is supposed to reassure me? I know perfectly well that whatever they are up to is anything but good.

# Chapter 19

# THE DOOMSDAY DEVICE

THE THRONG OF MASIES APPEARS expressionless, but with a closer look the corners of their lips seem to be bent into a smirk. It is as subtle as the Mona Lisa's smile, so I cannot be certain.

"Tell me why we should trust you when every single one of you has murdered a version of me and my parents."

"Or why we shouldn't just kill you all once we have Jon back," adds Beth.

"Well…" a Masie from the second row propels herself forward. "We all know how difficult it is to kill a person in this world. Unless a bullet is shot directly into someone's brain, they will recover. If you try roasting us with that flame-thrower one of you is hiding, the burns will surely hurt like hell, but we will heal. You could get around the healing properties by breaking our necks, but there are dozens of us."

"Why don't you tell them about that other thing?" another Masie snidely suggests.

"Oh yes. For every Masie you kill or attempt to harm, we will kill two of your people."

"We'll start with the children," a Masie in the front row announces. "Not because we're monsters, but because it's the smartest deterrent to an attack. We wouldn't feel joy after throwing a child from the platform in the sky, nor would we feel guilt. That young life lost way too soon would not be on us. It would be on each and every one of you."

I shake my head with disbelief. "You are monsters, no matter how you try to justify your actions."

Two of the Masies who left earlier return and are swiftly absorbed into the cluster.

"It's done," a voice says.

"Good," says Make-Up Masie.

"What is done?" Mom asks.

"We set up a contingency plan, Debra," replies Make-Up Masie. "We are more than aware of your intellect. You *could* find a way to kill us all and for that reason, we have set up a doomsday device to deter possible drastic action."

"A doomsday device?"

"Yes, Debra. If the time comes when not a single person with our DNA has a beating heart in the Garden, the doomsday device will activate. If you conjure up a clever plan to kill us all or drive us out of the Garden, doom will reign upon everyone here."

*Doom.*

I have had enough of that word for a lifetime.

"You know," I say, "for people who tell us they are our friends and that we should trust them, you sound a lot like supervillains."

"Is it possible, Mom?"

"Yes, Beth. I suppose it is." Mom is pondering the threat.

"Or they're bluffing," Beth adds.

"Or they're bluffing."

The two Masies who had entered the house return and give Make-Up Masie a nod.

"We have completed our tasks," Make-Up Masie says. "Once we let your friend go you are free to resume your lives. We have closed access to any lightways that will take you back to your home, Debra. The Tether World is also inaccessible."

*The Tether World?*

"Your children and the residents of the Garden are welcome to enter other lightways. We won't get in your way. Just pretend we're not here."

*Yeah, right.*

"That said," another Masie says, "the house is off limits to you now."

"If you need something," Make-Up Masie says, "knock and we will see if we can accommodate your request."

I try to resist the feeling of dread that passes through me. Despite Aunt Ruth's warning to keep them out of the Garden, could they be telling the truth? Even though they have murdered versions of my family, they might leave us alone if we do the same?

Ebby tugs on my sleeve. "It's him!"

A Masie comes forward from the back row, her arms tightly wrapped around the chest of a terrified Jon. She stops in front of Mom. "Before we hand over your friend, we have one additional demand."

"Tell us," Beth says through clenched teeth.

Masie eyes Mom, still clutching Jon. "Debra Wade must come with us."

# Chapter 20

# THE TRADE-OFF

"NO!" BETH AND I shout in unison.

Ebby starts to sob.

"You said you're not here to hurt us." I stand my ground, barely.

"We require your mother's expertise."

"We won't harm her," Make-Up Masie says.

*Do I detect a hint of sarcasm?*

"I'll come with you." Beth takes Mom's hand.

"No, I'll be fine. If you have a chance to go home, take it. Just get out of here."

Beth won't let go of Mom's hand.

"This isn't goodbye," Make-Up Masie says. "Come to the house and see your mother anytime."

Mom faces the army. "The boy," she demands. "Now."

"Of course."

Jon is released. He is clearly afraid to take even one step forward.

"Go on now. Flutter away little birdie."

He nearly tackles Ebby, both of them sniffling in each other's arms. Then he wraps his arms around me and Beth. "Thank you."

Ebby is frowning at the front of her blouse. "Dude, Target doesn't accept returns for tear stains."

I would normally laugh, but Mom is being taken away by these monsters. Things are only going to get worse. Mom glances back at us a couple of times before she enters the house.

The Garden residents chatter amongst themselves in small groups, picking up food wrappers and other litter from our meals. It calms their nerves and gives them time to realize that the danger is seemingly over. One group at a time, they quietly disperse. Soon, it's just me and Beth, and Ebby and Jon left in front of the house.

Ebby looks around the Garden and at the house. "So what now?"

Chapter 21

# LET THE RIGHT ONE IN

IN REDFERN, A CABIN like Cole's would sell for more than half a million, but ever since his death, it has remained empty. Nobody wanted to live in the home of a psychopath, not even the Creepers who were once devoted to him. As much as sleeping in Cole's cabin revolts me, it's a place where the four of us can spend the night without putting anyone out. We decide to sleep in the main room because the idea of sleeping in Cole's bed is disgusting.

If we were staying in a cabin like this in the real world, we would play games and have a fun night. But we aren't on vacation. We may not be locked in a room or roped to a chair, but we are prisoners, nonetheless.

Beth, Ebby, and Jon quickly fall asleep. Everything that's happened in the last few days keeps playing through my mind—the discovery of my aunt's true identity, the ambush at our house, the death of the woman who raised me, meeting Rose's husband, the friggin' monster in the valley and now, losing Mom to those evil women. How can Beth possibly sleep?

I roll onto my side and cough. Mucus has rapidly returned to my lungs. I cough again. And again.

What's happening? Did the Masies turn off the Garden's healing properties? I sit upright and hack non-stop. My chest is flaring, and little oxygen is making it through my clogged airways. I haven't taken my meds in two days so this is only going to get worse.

I reach out and tap Beth's shoulder. She rolls over, but I'm not looking into Beth's eyes. Masie's ambiguous Mona Lisa smile greets me. I leap to my feet, shrieking for Ebby and Jon, but they aren't there. In their place are two Masies, sporting non-committal sneers.

I run to the cabin door but a smirking Masie is blocking it. I run to the other bedroom, still hacking my lungs out. There is movement under the covers. The blankets and sheets are tossed aside and a figure crawls off the bed in a crab-like motion. It scampers towards me.

*Cole!*

"Don't worry, Synthia. I'll protect you." Cole's evil grin widens as he inches closer. His arms and legs are bent backwards like the possessed girl in *The Exorcist*.

I awaken with a jolt. Masie Winters is looming over me.

"I'm dreaming. You're not here." I'm breathless.

"You're not dreaming."

I bite my lip and the pain stuns me. Sometimes I bite my lip in dreams though, and it hurts just like it does now.

"When your friends wake up, bring them to the well in the Square." Masie swings open the front door and pauses, morning sunlight beaming into the room. Her threatening silhouette is blocking my escape. "See you soon." She shuts the door behind her, laughing.

I'm certain that I'm awake now. My lungs are clear. Beth, Ebby, and Jon are still asleep. Oh, how I envy them.

* * *

When we arrive at the Square, I'm surprised to see a lightway in front of the well. One Masie is waiting for us. Jon and Ebby are worried.

"What's happening?" Beth asks.

"We're expressing gratitude to your mother for her cooperation," Masie says.

I toss a reassuring look over my shoulder at Jon and Ebby. "What does that mean?"

"We're sending your friends home."

"Really? Just like that?" Beth is suspicious.

So am I.

"Ebby and Jon are free to go."

"We want to stay and help Beth and Syn," Jon protests.

"Brave boy." Masie flashes a toothy grin. "No, you will leave. Both of you."

There is nothing more to be said. It will be a relief to know that our friends are safe.

Masie watches our goodbyes closely.

"Should I try to get in touch with Luke?" Ebby whispers.

"No. We'll be okay." I don't really believe that, but Luke can't get into the Garden anyway. Even if he somehow managed to, the Masies would take out any aggression against them on the Garden residents. "Luke is building homes for people who are homeless. He is doing more in Haiti than he would be able to do here."

"If you say so." Ebby frowns. "Be careful."

Masie waves her arms impatiently. "Enough chatter. Time to go."

Jon is drowning in a puddle of tears as they fade into the lightway. He almost gets me going too. I wave goodbye and turn away as the lightway fades.

"I would like to see my mom," I say.

"Not today. She's busy."

"We'll be back tomorrow," says Beth firmly.

The next morning we're told that Mom is still busy. The following morning we're again told, "Not today, girls." Each morning we go to the house and knock on the door, and each morning we are told the same thing. We can see Mom through the window, sitting at a computer, but that doesn't stop us from worrying.

Three weeks go by, though it seems like three months. The Masies have kept their word and not caused any harm. They have been friendly and most people are used to seeing them roaming around. Most residents have resumed their normal lives because they no longer see our "visitors" as a threat.

*I know better.*

Beth and I do our part in the community. We pick fruit in the orchard and plant seeds in the vegetable garden. We pass on supply runs because those involve going to other worlds and we don't want to leave our mother.

Beth and Flint have become good friends. That is one thing that makes me happy, at least. At home, she didn't click with kids her age and spent her time with me and my friends. Lily and her best friend Nell have warmed up to me again. I enjoy spending time with them because it helps keep my mind off what's happening inside that house.

As the days pass, the cycle continues. Every morning, we're told that our mother is busy, and that she's fine. Then the door is shut in our faces.

Until today.

It's been thirty days since dozens of Masie Winters entered the Garden. This time, when the front door is opened, we are invited to come inside. We eye each other nervously.

We walk into the main room, where four Masies are sitting at computers.

"Syn."

"Yeah?" I follow Beth's eyes to the blood stains on the floor. My heart leaps.

The four Masies stand up. We are surrounded.

"Your mother hasn't been cooperating."

"She needs extra motivation."

Footsteps are stomping up the basement stairs now. Mom is shoved through the doorway by a Masie wearing a white lab coat that's splattered with blood. Tired and weak, Mom collapses.

We rush to her side.

"Mom!" I take one of her hands.

"What have they done to you?" Beth takes her other hand.

"Debra has been holding back."

Lab-Coat Masie kicks me in the stomach. Acid rises in my throat and I double over.

Meanwhile, Beth is kicking and screaming, trying to escape from the grips of two Masies.

"Will you cooperate now, Debra?" says Lab-Coat Masie. "Or do we continue?"

The pain in my stomach is fading thanks to the healing properties.

Beth is cursing. Mom still says nothing.

"We continue." Lab-Coat Masie takes a fistful of my hair and yanks me to my feet.

"Not that one. We are saving her for testing."

My attacker shoves me to the floor.

"Leave Beth alone!" I shout.

"Debra Wade?" my attacker says.

Mom shows no sign of compliance.

*Why isn't she helping us? She has done everything in her life to protect us.*

Beth is dragged to the center of the room by her hair, refusing to show any sign of discomfort. Her Masie reaches into a pocket and retrieves a metal ring with a blade protruding from the center.

Masie slips on the ring. "Last chance Debra."

Mom lowers her eyes.

Beth glares at her Masie without a trace of fear. Masie twists Beth around and holds her from behind, and with no hesitation, swipes the blade across Beth's throat.

# Chapter 22

# MOTHER,
# CAN YOU HEAR ME?

BETH GRASPS HER THROAT AND falls to her knees, blood spurting from the gash.

"No!" Mom is fighting to be freed from her Masie's grip.

My captor sets me free, laughing.

"Beth!" I press my hands against hers to try and stop the bleeding, but it doesn't make much difference. Beth pleads for help through glassy eyes.

"Do something!" Mom is still struggling with her Masie.

I whip off my shirt, fold it three times, and press it against my sister's neck.

The Masies are chuckling.

Suddenly, I remember the Garden's healing properties. Of course, she will be fine.

"You're going to be okay. Remember where we are."

I release the pressure on my bloodsoaked shirt and wait for an excruciating five seconds. The blood flow is a mere trickle now. The wound is healing! I smile over my shoulder at Mom.

"It will only get worse, Debra," Masie says. "Unless you help us."

Mom shakes her head, defiantly.

"If you kill Beth," Mom says, "you have no other leverage."

What about me? Why wouldn't they hurt me? Masie mentioned testing before. Testing for what?

"Oh, but Debra, because of your wonderful innovation we can torture her until the end of time." Masie towers over Mom triumphantly. "We will slit her throat again and again. We will do the same to Synthia if we decide to lop off young Bethany's head."

"Or, we can temporarily shut off the healing properties," says another Masie.

"You're animals!" Mom screams.

"You are the animal, allowing your kin to be tortured to satisfy your pride."

One Masie is coming downstairs, carrying a blouse. She tosses it on the floor in front of me and kicks my bloody shirt aside. "Put this on."

I pick up the white blouse, which is several sizes too big, and pull it over my head. It's either this or a bloodsoaked T-shirt.

"You okay?" I ask Beth.

"Yeah."

"Not for long, if your mother doesn't cooperate," another Masie interjects, then roughly escorts each of us to the middle of the room. Mom won't look at us.

*What is wrong with her?*

"Just a minute."

All eyes are on one of the Masies who's sitting at a computer terminal. The computer monitor in front of her turns white.

*I know what that means.*

A lightway stretches from the floor to the ceiling.

"In you go," Masie says, and shoves me into the light.

Everything immediately turns white. And by everything, I mean everything. It's just me and empty white space, known as the bubble. Sort of a room, if rooms didn't have walls and had cloud-like floors that look like you could fall through them.

*Where is Beth?*

As if someone is reading my mind, Beth is shoved in my direction, almost pushing me over. I catch her so she doesn't fall. Her throat hasn't started to bleed again. I still feel fine too.

"Beth, there must be healing properties here."

"Yeah. They can be turned on and off though."

Beth spent time here as Cole's prisoner, so she would know this.

"Let's hope they keep them on." I pause. "I don't know why Mom is letting them do this to us. Why doesn't she just tell them what they want to know?"

Beth sighs. "You know why."

She's right. I've been pushing the thought away, but there is really only one reason why Mom would let them hurt her children, the very same children she has dedicated the last twelve years of her life to protecting by doing horrible things. The alternative, whatever it is, must be even worse than what they are doing to us.

"If we can figure it out, they will too."

"They probably already have an idea, and when they put all the pieces together…" Beth checks out our surroundings, or lack of surroundings. "We need to get out of here."

"Don't suppose you have a plan?"

"Of course I do. It's a long shot, though."

"If a long shot is our only shot…"

Beth goes to the far side of the bubble, bends down and waves one arm around.

"What are you doing?"

"Remember when you rescued me from the bubble?"

"Of course."

"When you arrived here, I was gone."

"I thought I missed my opportunity to rescue you." Or even worse, that Cole had done something to her and she was beyond saving.

Beth continues to wave her arm through the white space. "When you had almost given up, I appeared."

My sister is practically narrating my thoughts. Suddenly, her arm disappears in mid-air.

"What the hell?" Before I can reach her side, she has pulled her arm back and it's visible again. I tap my hands up and down her arm to make sure it's real. "What happened to your arm?"

"When I was a prisoner here, I discovered a passage. One that I could enter from this bubble."

"Where does it go?"

"To another bubble."

I'm gobsmacked.

"That bubble has a secret passage too, leading to yet another bubble. And on and on until the passageways eventually stop."

"Why are there more bubbles?"

"It doesn't matter. What does matter is that through each of the other bubbles there is an exit—a voidway. I exited when I was trapped here."

"Where did it take you?"

"To a house. Not the same house we just came from. A house in another Garden."

*There are other Gardens!*

"If a voidway has been left open in one of the bubbles, we can escape through it."

"And go home!"

"Well…" Beth's voice grows quiet. "An open voidway will give us access to another Garden and then we could exit and yes, go to a home. But it wouldn't be *our* home."

So many questions and possibilities. The multiverse I thought I knew has grown beyond my expectations. "How can escaping from one of these bubbles help us if it doesn't take us home?"

"We can get help and find weapons to fight off the Masies. Or…"

"Right. It gives us options."

"We have to be careful though."

"Because?"

"The other bubbles might not have healing properties. And without them…"

"Your throat will start bleeding again."

"I could die."

"I will go," I say. "I'll search the other bubbles for a voidway."

But—"

"If the voidway leads to a house in another Garden, that Garden might have healing properties. And then, I'll come back for you. They won't even be watching us on the monitor because they don't know that we know about the other bubbles. They believe that we are trapped with nowhere else to go. We have that much going for us."

Beth frowns. "You're sick though. You haven't taken any pills or done treatments for a month."

"I have something to live for. My little sister is depending on me. I can do this."

"I wish you would stop calling me your little sister." Beth smiles through the tears that are streaming down her cheeks. I wipe them aside with my thumbs and gently take her face in my hands.

"I'll be fine." I have to put on a brave face or she won't let me go. "Tell me what to do and I'll be back before you know it."

## Chapter 23

# YOU!

HOLDING BETH'S HAND TIGHTLY, I stretch one leg into the space she is pointing to. Her hand slips from mine and I'm suspended in desolation. It looks and feels like the same bubble, except Beth is not here and I feel ill. My lungs are filling up with phlegm at a startling rate.

As Beth instructed, I squint my eyes to discern any sign of a faint light. There is no evidence of a voidway.

Coughing uncontrollably, I cross the white space and frantically wave my hands around, searching for a passageway into the next bubble. All hope seems lost until my forearm disappears.

*Yes!*

I stretch a leg forward and step into the next bubble. More white nothingness, and more coughing. My lung function is deteriorating with every passing second, my heart is pounding, and I'm lightheaded from lack of oxygen.

I am tempted to go back, but Beth is counting on me.

I'm unsuccessful in searching for a voidway and I barely make it to the next bubble.

I squint, face disappointment, find the next passageway, then move on. This continues through six more bubbles, before I collapse.

This search isn't just for my survival. It's for Beth's and Mom's. Even if it's a long shot, I have to keep trying.

I cough up blood, which is always a bad sign. If the next bubble doesn't have a voidway or healing properties, I will have to go back to Beth. Otherwise, I will collapse again and never get up. I'm of no use to anyone dead. Plus, Beth will come after me and bleed to death.

Stumbling across the empty white space, still hacking up blood, I stretch my foot into the next bubble. My imagination offers comfort with the memory of Beth's hand in mine. But entering the next bubble brings despair as I visualize Beth's hand slipping from mine again. I collapse face down on the ground (or whatever the white "surface" is beneath me). I remind myself that is the last one. If there is no voidway or healing properties, I must turn around.

*Breathe in, breathe out.*

The more I breathe, the easier it is. The coughing has stopped and my lungs are clearing up. I suddenly feel good. Really good. The healing properties are functioning in this bubble.

I stand up carefully, peering through the whiteness for a voidway, hope quickly fading.

Then, something catches my attention.

A hooded figure in a black robe is sitting on a small wooden stool, just twenty feet away. It rises from the stool slowly. My chest pain is gone, but it's been replaced by dread. The figure approaches and stops barely two inches from me. I carefully slip off the hood and gasp.

*It can't be!*

I am looking into my own eyes. But these eyes are bloodshot. This face is scarred and the skin is bubbling like boiling soup, despite the healing properties. This is the face of someone whose death I witnessed. Someone who died *because* of me.

*Synister.*

# Chapter 24

# PAST SYNS

SOMETHING IS DIFFERENT FROM WHEN I first met Synister. She was angry and full of hate, while this Synister is calm and vulnerable.

"Synister?"

"What did you say?" Her confusion is surprising, her breath foul.

"Synister. Does that mean anything to you?"

"No. I saw you die. I saw *all* of you die."

"Who is keeping you prisoner?" I ask.

"You know who," she replies.

"Humor me."

"Our dear old mom and dad." She looks away.

I think I've got it. In this alternate Garden, Mom and Dad were not held captive by Synister. She very likely never even met Cole, so the events that transpired for me—Cole coming to my world, bringing me to the Garden, holding me prisoner, and attempting to do a mad experimental procedure on me—never happened.

In this Synister's Garden, there is no version of me to accidentally cause Synister's death. In my Garden, she is the last surviving Syn, ripped from her world to be experimented on in an attempt to find a cure for me. She is also still a prisoner. Or at least until alt-Mom and Dad's experiments eventually kill her.

"Not *our* Mom and Dad. You were taken from your parents, right?"

Synister nods.

"I'm from another world. Where I come from, I…we have a sister."

"A sister?"

"Beth."

Synister attempts to comprehend everything I've told her. "How did you get here?"

"Beth and I are being held prisoner in another bubble."

Her singed eyebrows rise.

"Beth discovered a way to escape from one bubble to another. Believe it or not, there are more bubbles just like this."

"So we can get out of here?" She sounds hopeful.

"We were hoping I would find a voidway, which is basically an exit through another bubble." I'll go back and bring Beth here and when your captors bring you a meal, we'll attack them and escape through your Garden."

"Does your Garden have healing properties?"

"Yes."

"We should go to your Garden."

"Why?"

"Some sort of beast has invaded our Garden. A monster. The Garden isn't what it was before. They've kept me in here since the thing began its rampage. All their plans have gone to hell. The house is destroyed, along with the machine that creates the healing properties. Ian and Deb open this bubble from the sewers every few days to bring me food and water. They don't know what to do with me."

An empty plate and water bottle are lying on the floor. Ian and Deb are due for another visit. Maybe, just maybe, Beth and I can get out before she bleeds to death and I drop dead, escape the monster, and go home through a lightway in this Synister's Garden. Except that not only would we be leaving Mom behind, Synister couldn't come with us because she'd die in our world before we could get her to a hospital. So, we'd either be leaving her in this bubble, or in a world with her captors, that damn monster and no healing properties.

"The thing is," I tell her, "while the bubble that Beth and I are trapped in has healing properties, the ones in between don't. We have to travel through nine bubbles, getting sicker and sicker on the way."

Her face falls. "I still want to come with you."

"I barely made it here."

"I am willing to try for a second chance at life. Or I will die trying and can finally be at peace. Either way is better than living like this."

Like the Synister I knew, this one is in constant pain from all the diseases my parents injected into her. She is fine with dying if it puts an end to her pain. I am not okay with that. Another Synister will not die on my watch. I will do my damnedest to save her.

I fill her in on Masie Winters and her army, and about Mom being held captive and refusing to help with their experiments. We discuss the amount of time it will take to get through each bubble and how to proceed to the next one. I tell her about everything we will have to do to have any chance of escaping the bubbles and returning to the Garden Beth and I came from.

Of course my symptoms will resurface with a vengeance right after exiting this bubble, but I'm hopeful I can make it if I move quickly. I'm committed because Beth is counting on me.

Synister, on the other hand, has more than cystic fibrosis to contend with. Her numerous diseases are so severe that even the healing properties can't fight the symptoms fast enough to keep them at bay. When I destroyed the healing properties in my world, the other Synister dropped to the ground instantly and drew her last breath a minute later.

Of course, I don't tell her about how I accidentally killed another version of her in a fit of rage. I emphasize the danger. She is perfectly aware.

After I have gotten her up to speed, I pick up the wooden stool and slam it against the cloudy white surface. One of the legs snaps off as if it had been smashed against a concrete floor. I slam it repeatedly until all four legs have broken off. There is a metal plate at the top of each leg and a nail protruding from one of them. I decide to hold the one with the nail and slide each of the other legs into a pocket. They stick out, but my oversized blouse covers them nicely.

I have just finished wrapping a strip we tore from the bottom of her robe over my nose and mouth. Because cystic fibrosis patients have weakened immune systems, we are warned to not interact with others who have cystic fibrosis to avoid passing germs or bacteria to one another. With Synister having so many diseases, I need to play it safe where there are no healing properties.

"You can do this," I tell her.

"I'm not certain I will survive, but there is a chance I can fight through this and make it to the other bubble with healing properties. While you have the love for your sister as motivation, I will use the chance to meet her as mine. I also have a shot at getting out of here and living in a Garden without being experimented on. I have everything to gain and honestly, nothing to lose."

She is right. And it is her decision to make.

"Alright," Synister says, getting into position. "Let's do this."

# Chapter 25

# HOODWINKED

I MOVE THROUGH THE FIRST passageway into the next bubble and my health immediately starts to deteriorate. Synister stumbles behind me to the next passageway. As planned, she goes through first.

Synister is coughing terribly. I'm feeling lousy, but she is much sicker and growing weaker. She is forcing herself to hurry, but her efforts are draining any energy she has left.

At the halfway point of the sixth bubble, Synister's knees buckle. I catch her, but barely have the strength to hold her up.

"Three more bubbles and you live," I say in between coughs. "You stop now, you die."

She nods and forces herself to her feet. There is something about the will to live that gives you a boost of adrenaline. If she is in the same condition the other Synister was in when I destroyed the Garden's healing properties, she should be dead. Yet, knowing that she is so close to a new lease on life, something inside keeps her going.

When we enter the second-to-last bubble, I feel near death's door. Synister collapses. Will to live or not, one's body can only handle so much. I kneel down to her. One of the blisters on her cheek bursts, and then another. Blood and puss ooze down both cheeks.

"Wasn't meant to be," she says in a barely audible whisper.

"Like hell!"

*I let her die once. It won't happen again.*

I clasp her hand and with a surprising burst of vigor, haul her to the next passageway. She isn't breathing. I lift her by the shoulders and drag her through to the bubble with precious healing properties, and where Beth awaits.

I heave a sigh of relief, remove the cloth from my face, and take a deep breath.

"You're back!" Beth dashes over. "What the hell?"

"She's not our enemy. She's a victim, like us."

Beth is not convinced. "Are *you* okay?"

"I'm feeling better already."

Synister still isn't breathing. Neither was Luke when he was bleeding out from that bullet, but he was revived when we got him to a spot with healing properties.

I lean Synister's head against my body. "C'mon Syn. This is your chance at a new life. Your chance to live. C'mon." I use the cloth to wipe pus and blood off her face. Her vacant eyes suggest that I must accept the truth.

"Syn, she's gone."

"She was just alive. She was…so close."

A tear trickles down my face and falls into one of her eyes. She blinks!

"Am I dead?" she whispers.

"No," I say through a mess of tears.

The sickness is still fighting through the healing properties, though she manages to sit up. "You saved me." She smiles weakly. "Thank you."

"You'll live to see another day." I grin.

"I have a sister," she says, glancing at Beth.

"No," Beth gestures in my direction, "*she* has a sister. We needed weapons, not another Synister."

"Why do you call me that?" Synister asks.

"It's a long story," I tell her. "For now, we have other more important business. I hand them each a stool leg. "It isn't much, but this might be enough to get us out of the house."

"Okay," Beth says, happy to see that I brought something to fight back with. "Don't suppose you have a plan?"

"As a matter of fact, I do."

* * *

I am the first to admit that my plan is far-fetched, but that doesn't make it a bad plan. Another long shot, yeah. But it's the only idea we've got.

With Synister already informed, I lay out the plan for Beth. My other allows me to rip the hood off her robe. I fold it three times and hand it to Beth to use as a bandage for her neck. I take the cloth I had just worn as a mask and wrap it around Beth's neck to keep the makeshift bandage in place. Once we leave the house, we will escape through a lightway. Beth's neck will certainly begin bleeding as soon as we enter a new world. This should keep the bleeding at bay until we can get her medical attention.

Synister and I remove our clothes. I put on her robe and boots while she slips into my runners, khakis, and oversized blouse.

Now, I hide. To the best of my ability, anyway. It's not like there is a couch or a filing cabinet to crouch behind. I step into the first bubble I escaped to and peek back through to see what is happening. Even though most of my body is in a bubble with no healing properties, I feel fine. The healing properties in the first bubble must be saving me.

Now it's time to put the really crazy part of the plan into action. Wearing my clothes, Synister drops to her knees and pretends to be in pain. Beth tries to console her. The idea is to wait for Masie and Co. to see this on the monitor and freak out because my face is bubbling. After all, they didn't want me to be harmed in the first place. Although, if they have been watching us coordinate this entire time, our plan is shot.

We wait for probably fifteen minutes. I hope Beth and Synister can keep this up. Suddenly, there is immense pain in my head. It feels like someone has pierced my skull with a knife. Then, sharp pain in my stomach. I can hardly move because the pain is so intense. Being partly in a bubble with healing properties and in one without must be causing problems. I have to come out of hiding and go back to the first bubble immediately!

Just as I force my limbs to move and manage to push my upper chest through, one of the Masies appears.

She crouches to examine Synister. "What happened here?"

"I don't know," Beth says in a fake panic. She reaches for the stool leg in her back pocket.

I crawl out of the other bubble and vomit.

Masie looks up. "What the hell?"

Before Masie can stand, Beth slams the metal part of the stool leg into her forehead until she collapses.

Beth helps me up. "You okay?"

"Ugh. I will be."

"Let's get out of here. Let me help you."

Just as Beth is leading us through the voidway, another Masie appears and pushes her backwards, knocking me sideways.

Beth retaliates quickly and pierces the nail on her stool leg into that Masie's foot. She shrieks so horribly I feel like vomiting again. Beth pulls it out and impales her other foot. Masie staggers and reaches down to nurse her injuries, giving Beth a chance to find the voidway again.

She waves her hands around frantically.

*What if they have already shut it after seeing what we did?*

I'm relieved when Beth's arm disappears. "Let's go!"

I waste no time, with Synister close behind.

There are three Masies in the house, one of which is on the ground being pummeled by Beth. She doesn't waste any time. Lundy is huddled in a corner, frightened and confused. Mom is lying on the floor, bloody and bruised.

I swing my weapon at one Masie's head, but she grabs my wrist and squeezes with such a vice-like grip the wind is knocked out of me. My weapon falls.

"You!" Synister's raspy voice rises behind me. She lunges at Mom and wraps her hands around her throat. "You murdering bitch!"

I scream as Mom's face begins to lose color.

Chapter 26

# FRIENDS AND FOES

OUR PLAN HAS BEEN BLOWN to hell by Synister's betrayal. She knows this isn't the Debra Wade who experimented on her and yet she's totally lost it and is taking revenge any way she can.

The attack on Mom garners the attention of the two Masies left standing. Synister fights to keep her hands around Mom's throat as they attempt to pry her off. The stool leg is knocked from her pocket and as one of the Masies reaches for it, Synister mouths one word to me: sorry.

Who knows what they will do to Synister? Beth and I have no way to save her now. We either run while they're distracted or end up trapped in the bubble again. So, we make a beeline for the back door.

My wrist is grabbed as I step outside. Beth whips out her weapon and drives the nail into Masie's hand, then takes my hand and we bolt down the stairs.

Was this Synister's plan all along or did she see Mom and just lose control? Either way, I feel terrible leaving her. There is no way to save Mom right now, but she should be safe as long as they need her expertise. As for Synister....

We sprint through the Garden, passing by confused humans and Creepers. I trail behind Beth as best I can, our path zigzagging and my long robe whipping from side to side, tripping me every few steps.

"We have to get you a new outfit!" Beth shouts between breaths.

Two Masies are catching up. We need to get to the fog and lose them so we can figure out our next move.

Just as we reach the border of the fog, I trip on my robe and fall flat on my face, yelping with surprise. A foot comes down heavy on my back.

Beth skids to a stop, but before she can use her weapon, a Masie knocks it from her hand.

"You two are not going anywhere!"

"Who was that deformed girl? You'll tell us this instant."

My attacker lets out a bloodcurdling scream and the foot lifts off my back. I flip over, only to be greeted by the gruesome sight of one of those half dog, half crocodile Creepers chewing on her leg. She kicks free, but her head jerks back and she catapults to the grass, squirming around like she's still being attacked.

*What is happening?*

A second Creeper dog is clinging to the other Masie's leg. I am startled as her head jerks back and she lands on the grass too. Both Masies are out cold.

Crystal appears, in the flesh, of course. Breathless from running, I can only nod my appreciation.

The Creeper dogs gallop over to Beth, their eager greeting almost knocking her over. She laughs and points to me. One of them pounces, tongue hanging out of its long croc-like mouth, pleading for affection. As I desperately try to keep the scaly critter from licking my face, I am relieved by the sight of Lundy approaching.

"Let's get into the fog before more come!" he says. "We need to talk."

Leaving the Creeper dogs behind, Beth, Lundy, Crystal, and I head to protective fog cover and huddle together. I fill them in.

"But there are dozens of them," Lundy finally says. "Nice robe, by the way."

"You know me, the queen of fashion," I reply with an eyeroll. "I know there are a lot of them. We'll just hide."

Crystal shakes her head. "They'll eventually find you."

"We have to save our mom," Beth says.

"Right," I add. "We have to come up with a plan to get her out of that house."

"You guys and your plans." Lundy shakes his head. "Syn, have you ever noticed that your plans never go down like they're supposed to?"

"That thought has crossed my mind."

"We're not leaving without Mom," Beth says.

"Right. We aren't going anywhere ju—"

Something smacks my back and I'm lifted and flung through the air. Everything is a blur. I can barely make out Beth swinging beside me.

*Maya! What the hell is she doing?*

We are lifted higher in the fog and swung from treetop to treetop. My body painfully collides with a tree branch. By the time the healing properties provide comfort, I'm smacking into another branch. The robe is flapping around my feet.

In the distance, lightways appear and disappear. We're moving towards them. I'd scream to stop Maya but it's impossible to catch my breath. Not that she'd listen anyway. And now I'm freefalling to the ground, with Beth alongside me.

*Is this it? Is Maya killing us for allowing the Masies into the Garden?*

My fall is halted abruptly when I am just inches above ground. I'm bouncing up and down as if attached to a bungee cord. Finally, my feet touch the ground and I hobble around good and dizzy, with Maya's web still attached to my back.

"What the hell, Maya?" I scream. My voice sounds muffled inside my head because my ears haven't popped yet. A lightway disappears and another one opens.

"Your mother made me promise to get you out of the Garden."

"No!" I swallow hard and my ears are finally un-blocked. "We have to save my mom. Please help us."

"I'm not leaving without my sister. I'm not leaving without my mother." Maya mocks me. "Your dedication to your loved ones gets other families killed. I know that better than anyone."

*That stings.*

"We're staying." Beth is defiant.

"That is not what your mother wants."

Maya shoots a strand of web up a tree and lifts us both with her.

"No!" Beth shrieks.

"Your mother asked me for this favor." Maya looks down at us. "This is the first and last one. Go start a new life. Do whatever you wish."

She drops to the ground with us in tow, landing in front of a steady lightway. "If you return to the Garden, you are dead to me."

She shoves us into the light.

# Chapter 27

# TOMORROWLAND

I ASSESS OUR NEW SURROUNDINGS and realize we are in a Redfern quite unlike the one we live in.

Most of the houses and farmland that would be in our Redfern are gone. Instead, there are greenhouses for as far as the eye can see.

We walk between two structures, peering through hazy glass at the machines tending to crops.

It's freezing cold and I'm glad to still be wearing Synister's robe. I start coughing. My lungs are clogging up again.

"I'll be okay." I try to reassure my sister.

We hurry to the front of the property. An odd vehicle is operating outside the greenhouses. It looks like a greenhouse on wheels. Harvested ears of corn, totally out of season, are piled in a heap. The vehicle is moving despite there being no driver. It's like we've traveled to the future.

Beth places one hand on my back as I double over, hacking. "Let's find..." She trails off and grasps her neck where it had been slashed. Blood is soaking through the fabric!

I apply pressure to her bandage but my coughing fit worsens, as does the pain in my chest. *We need help!*

"C'mon, Beth!" My breath rasps in my throat but my words are still understood.

She follows me to the road where a row of futuristic vehicles are parked. We approach a bright red smart car. It has two passenger seats, yet like the others, it lacks a steering wheel. A touchscreen is attached to the dash. There are no handles on the doors.

I tug on the decrepit sign for 9078 Patten Road. If I can gather enough strength to pry it off, it can be used to break a window. I pull and pull and am forced to stop for another coughing fit. It feels like my chest is going to explode. I have to hold on tightly to remain standing, but a sliver of wood stabs my hand and I lose my balance. Beth is still trying to stop the bleeding from the gash in her throat but her bloodstained hands prove that she is failing.

I press my hands against the concrete and try to sit up. Without treatment, my lungs will fail soon.

While crawling over to Beth, dread paralyzes me at the sound of approaching footsteps. A woman is running over to us. She's in her early twenties and bundled up in reflective winter outerwear. Within seconds she's at my side. I can't speak.

"It's okay," she says calmly. "My name is Abby."

"Sister...." I point to Beth.

Abby helps Beth to her feet and escorts her to the car. "Back door open," she says.

She helps Beth lie down on a flat plastic surface behind the two front seats, and then comes to help me. Though this stranger can't be much bigger than I am, she lifts me into the car beside Beth. "I'll take care of the rest. Your sister needs your help now."

Blood is dripping down Beth's neck and her eyes are glassy. I'm terrified of losing her.

*I can't move!*

"Your sister is depending on you." Abby snaps her fingers and gives me a shake. "Can you hear me?"

I nod, quickly coming to my senses.

"Good girl!" She dives onto the front seat and fastens her seatbelt.

I spread my hands securely around Beth's neck and try to summon strength. Blood is already seeping down my wrists.

*Hold on Beth!*

"Hospital!" Abby says. "Level-red emergency."

"Level-red emergency," a female voice echoes.

The car speaks! And drives itself! I don't hear so much as a hum from the engine as we speed down the road.

"We will arrive at Redfern Memorial in two minutes and forty-two seconds," the car announces.

In my world, the hospital is at least a five-minute drive from my house. The car must be driving faster than it seems.

"Hang on!" Abby says.

We arrive at the hospital just as quickly as the car said we would. Two hospital attendants pry my cramped hand away from Beth's neck and place her on a stretcher. Her eyes are still glassy. She's on the brink of death. My concern is so great, I barely realize I am on the brink too before I….

* * *

I groggily open my eyes. The room is nothing like the ones at Redfern Memorial, which in my world I have gotten to know too well over the years. Here, I am surrounded by glass walls that separate my room from other rooms, all of them empty.

There is some sort of machine to the left of my bed. It's a thin, vertical, shiny white platform with several red and green lights on it. A touchscreen is attached to it like a fridge magnet.

My chest is congested but no worse than on a good day at home. They haven't inserted an IV drip or an oxygen tube and there is no IV apparatus in the room.

I swing my feet over the side of the bed. A loud buzzing sound erupts from the mysterious machine and the touchscreen lights up, displaying a photo of a meadow and the time: 9:34 A.M.

I was here all night.

*Where is Beth?*

The buzzing stops when my feet touch the cold floor.

"Please remain in your bed," says the machine. "An attendant will arrive in five seconds."

The machine's voice sounds like the voice in the smart car—like there is a real person in this room, not a digital robot. Sure enough, in mere seconds a young man wearing a white coat hurries into my room.

"My sister…"

*What?*

Beth floats into the room behind the man, hovering above the floor in a black recliner. Her neck isn't bandaged. There is a thin white line where the gash had been.

I leap out of bed. The man in the white coat moves aside so I can hug Beth.

"You look amazing."

"Don't I always?" She smirks. "You too."

"Is this—?"

"Yes, Redfern Memorial," the man confirms. "Please return to your bed. The doctor will be with you shortly."

I sit on the side of my bed and after the man leaves, Beth's chair floats over. She is controlling it with a tablet.

"Beth, did we travel to…"

"The future? No." She holds up the tablet.

Right beside the time, today's date is also displayed at the top of the screen.

"Wow. The technology here surpasses what we have at home. I shouldn't feel this well so quickly, and the gash on your throat has been miraculously superglued shut."

Beth laughs. "The doctor told me he used a biological surgical glue, which will absorb within a week. He promises that if there is a scar, it will barely be noticeable."

"This is insane. I thought you were going to die."

"I guess we lucked out."

"You're telling me."

After some lighthearted banter, we talk about what occurred in the Garden.

"I'm sure Mom is alive," Beth says.

"What if they figure out what they've been trying to beat out of her? Or, what if she tells them what they want to know now that they can't hurt us?"

"Don't think like that."

I also can't help but think the worst about Synister. Despite her betrayal, I feel terrible that I let her down.

*Again.*

The doctor arrives with a young man who doesn't look much older than me. The doctor is wearing typical attire, while the young man is wearing beige khakis and a brown sweater. The fashion here hasn't evolved as much as technology has.

The doctor introduces herself as Dr. Sharma. The young man is Dr. Lee, a resident. He must be older than he looks.

Dr. Sharma picks up the tablet beside my bed and silently reads the screen for a minute. "Beth has been cleared for release as soon as we have her information processed. She is almost as good as new. No follow-up visits are necessary."

*Wow!*

"You, on the other hand, Ms. Wade…" She pauses. "Your first name?

"Synthia." If I'm alive in this world, I'll be in their system.

She taps the screen a few times, glances at the resident and at me, frowning. "Ms. Wade, you are a bit of a mystery."

"Why is that?" My stomach is flipping, big time.

"Are you aware of your condition?"

"Of course. Cystic fibrosis."

"Right." She eyes me curiously. "This has been quite a shock to our staff."

"Why is that?" Beth speaks, because I can't.

"Because, a cure for cystic fibrosis was discovered decades ago."

# Chapter 28

# THE CURE

*A CURE? I MUST BE DREAMING.*

"Like Parkinson's, multiple sclerosis, and countless other one-time terminal illnesses," Dr. Sharma says, "cystic fibrosis has been eradicated in all developed countries. Or so we believed, until now."

My jaw drops.

"Synthia?" Dr. Sharma says.

"Uh huh?"

"Where are you from?"

"Vancouver," Beth blurts. "Will that be a problem?"

"Of course not. We have a health and wellness accord with Canada."

"I don't understand," the resident says with an accusatory tone. "The treatment to cure you of CF would have been available to you in Vancouver." He turns to Dr. Sharma. "And yet she's suggesting they weren't even aware of it?"

"We'll discuss that later," Dr. Sharma replies. "Synthia should rest."

The resident is noticeably agitated, but nods.

Dr. Sharma puts the tablet back in its rightful place. "We will have a cot sent in for you, Beth, so you can stay with your sister."

"Thank you."

"And your parents?" asks the resident.

"I called and left a message," says Beth.

"Get some rest, Synthia. I'll check on you in a while."

As soon as the two doctors leave, the tablet attached to the machine lights up. "A bed will arrive in one minute and forty-six seconds."

"What service!" Beth smiles widely. "Plus, *a cure!*"

"Yeah." I detach the tablet and tap the screen, preoccupied with uncertainty.

"Is there something I can help you with?" the computer asks.

"Tell me about the cure for cystic fibrosis."

I choose to read the information rather than have it recited. While Beth and I are reading, the glass door slides open and a cot wheels in, a low humming sound emanating from a switchboard at its foot. It parks against the wall, two feet from my bed.

"Oh no." Beth calls my attention back to the tablet.

"What?"

"There's an eight-month treatment period. The procedure was discovered by researchers at the Jasper Medical Research Centre," she reads aloud. She continues to read to me about how the procedure has cured not just cystic fibrosis and the diseases Dr. Sharma listed. A cure has been found for most terminal diseases, even cancer.

This is incredible. All the lives saved. All the suffering that has been prevented. I mean, CF takes way too many lives, but cancer is something that gets most people at some point if something else doesn't get them first. People like…

*Janna.*

I hold the tablet up to my mouth, knowing full well I could speak to it from across the room. "Look up Janna Larson. Janna Larson in West Linn, Oregon."

"There is no Janna Larson in West Linn, Oregon. There are eighty-four Janna Larsons in the United States."

I am soon disappointed that none of the Janna Larson profile photos even closely resembles my dearly departed friend.

"Look up Linda Larson in West Linn, Oregon."

A profile for Janna's mom immediately appears and I hungrily scan through the info. My heart sinks.

"I'm sorry," Beth says.

According to this world's records, Janna's mother married another man. They have two sons and no daughters. In this world where cancer has been cured, Janna was never born.

"It's not fair." Determined, I ask the tablet to look up one more name in this world: Synthia Wade.

The information provided is grim. Synthia Wade and her parents were murdered when she…I…was only seven.

*By Masie Winters, of course.*

Damn her. My other could have been cured in this world—perhaps she was—yet Masie killed her, stealing her chance at a long and healthy life.

Beth has something on her mind. "They'll figure out we're not from Canada. They probably already have."

"I know."

"Maybe it's a long shot," she rests her hand on my arm, "but it's possible they still might treat you."

"That *is* a long shot."

"But Syn, if you have that chance…if you could be cured…maybe you should think about it."

"If we stay here longer than a couple of days, we risk the lightway closing on us and never being able to save Mom."

"There might not be a way to save Mom," Beth says, surprising me.

"Beth…"

"I want to save her more than anything. But you know what Mom would want."

Mom would want what she has always wanted. What she sacrificed her soul trying to achieve. Debra Wade would want me to be cured.

"I want what Mom wants. For you to live until we're both old and crabby, and cold all the time,"

Beth says. "We could start a new life here and never have to worry about Masie Winters again."

"But Mom…and the people in the Garden…"

"I know. It would kill me to never know if Mom is okay. To never see her again and know that she is worried about us. But it would torture me to lose you. Think about it. But get some rest first."

Ready to obey the doctor's orders, I lie back and drift off, still clasping Beth's hand. As I am about to enter dreamland, I force myself to stay awake. Against my better judgement, I do what Beth suggests.

I think about it.

Chapter 29

# THE BREACH

THERE IS NO TELLING HOW long I was asleep, but gradually my eyes adjust to the light. Beth's cot is empty, and a mountain of a man in a security guard getup is leaning against the glass wall next to the door.

*I don't like this.*

"Excuse me, Sir."

"You are excused," the machine reports, with a subtle slyness in its feminine tone.

I sigh. My chest is as congested as usual, but nothing serious. As I stand up, a woman in a black suit—fit, with short black hair, mid-30s—passes the security guard outside my room. The door slides open and she enters.

"Where is my sister?" I ask calmly, not wanting to start off on the wrong foot with whoever this is.

"She's fine. Please sit or lie down. Whatever makes you comfortable."

Two uniformed police officers enter. The female cop comes over to me and the male officer remains in front of the glass door, as if to block it.

I'm sitting on the edge of my bed. Though panicked, especially since Beth is not here, I must keep a friendly exterior. There is no reason to antagonize these people.

"How are you feeling?" the suited woman asks.

"Okay. Are you a doctor?" I know very well that she is not.

"I am Special Agent Galani."

*Special agent? FBI? Crap.*

"I have a few questions for you," Galani says. "Starting with your name."

"Synthia W—"

Galani holds up her hand. "Synthia Wade died ten years ago. Again, what is your name?"

"Synthia Wade. From Canada."

"There is no Synthia Wade in Canada. Not even with the common spelling."

"I, uh, don't know what to say."

"I'm sure you don't." Any hint of a smile is gone. "Your DNA matches the Synthia Wade who died here at age seven. She did not have a sister."

I say nothing. Best to let her fill me in on what she thinks.

"Why don't you tell me where you are really from?"

I open my mouth—

"Not the country, the world."

*She knows about the multiverse?*

"What world?" I ask, with faux confusion.

"Stop playing games. I am aware you are not from this world. So before you really piss me off, tell me what world you came from and where the breach into this world is located."

*The breach? Does she mean the lightway?*

"I don't know."

Galani says nothing. I look away. She motions to the officers outside the room and they move aside, allowing Dr. Sharma to enter. The doctor nods to Galani as she approaches.

"This is what is going to happen," Galani says, not even acknowledging Dr. Sharma. "The doctor will give you a final assessment. I will interview you again and if you continue to be uncooperative..." she pauses, "just trust me, young lady. It will be better if you cooperate."

*That sounds like a threat.*

After the doctor asks how I am feeling, she scans the tablet beside my bed. The machine must have been assessing my health the entire time. Incredible.

"Her health is moderate," the doctor tells Galani. "She will require continued treatment. I have shared her records with Homeland Security."

Galani is watching me closely.

"Take care, Synthia." The doctor smiles sincerely, but with concern, and exits the room.

"Now," Galani says, "let me tell you a little about this world you and your sister have breached. You already know that the Synthia Wade of this world is dead. She and her parents were murdered. What your web search didn't tell you was that she was killed by a woman named Masie Winters."

*Holy crap. They know this?*

"Shortly after the Wades were killed, we became aware that Winters had discovered a multiverse and breached parallel worlds. That put this murder investigation on the radar of Homeland Security. We fear regular breaches could lead to parallel worlds mining our resources, stealing our technology, and leading us into war. This should help you realize why we are concerned about breaches."

"Have there been any breaches so far?"

"There have been several, aside from the original breach, and yours. You are an alternate of one of the victims of the first breach. So, I think you can see how that is quite the coincidence."

"Yes."

"Is there a Masie Winters in the world you come from?"

*What do I say? That she practically raised me?*

"Did Masie Winters send you here? Did she enter this world with you?"

"Slow down. I'll answer your questions."

"That is wise."

"I will answer your questions, after you let me see my sister."

"Your sister is on her way to the precinct."

"Take me there. I need to see that she's okay."

"You aren't in charge here." Galani's eyes narrow. "You will answer my questions and when your sister cooperates, your request will be granted."

BOOM!

The building shakes from some sort of explosion. An alarm sounds as smoke fills the hallway. Galani and I watch the panic in the corridors through the glass walls.

I chuckle. Galani thinks Beth will cooperate?

*She doesn't know my sister.*

# Chapter 30

# MANHUNT

HOVERING ABOVE THE FLOOR IN a chair like the one Beth was sitting in, I am escorted by Galani through the melee in the corridor. Unlike Beth's chair, this one is not under my control. It drives itself, seemingly aware of where we are going. Other patients hover beside me in similar chairs, accompanied by panicked hospital staff determined to evacuate the building.

I'm coughing from the smoke, though not affected as badly as usual.

We exit the hospital and cross the parking lot, gathering with others on a strip of grass alongside the road.

There is no sign of Beth.

Driverless emergency vehicles speed into the parking lot. Police officers and firefighters analyze the situation and consult with hospital staff and security. Two firefighters eventually enter the building.

Galani speaks to someone through a Bluetooth device in her ear. "I'm at the south end of the parking lot with the eldest Wade girl. Bring the sister to me."

There's a pause. Galani's eyebrows furrow. "What?"

BOOM!

A car parked halfway down the block explodes and fire engulfs the interior. Galani's attention is diverted. She doesn't notice my chair floating back to the parking lot.

BOOM!

Another car explodes.

The explosions distract Galani while my chair carries me to the back of a white van. My chair halts and the back door opens.

"Get in!"

"Beth!"

Galani is racing this way. I leap from my chair and climb inside the van.

"Drive!" The back doors slam shut and the van accelerates at Beth's command.

"Wow." I try to keep my balance as we speed away, mere seconds before Galani arrives.

"I programmed the GPS," Beth says. "You okay?"

"I am now."

"Good. Put these on." She tosses me a pair of jeans, a red T-shirt with the @ symbol printed on the front, and a pair of sneakers, presumably swiped from some teenage girl's hospital room.

"Was all this necessary?" I ask, while slipping on the jeans beneath my hospital robe. "They just wanted information."

"I overheard the police say that we would be handed over to Jasper Incorporated's security team after they got the information they wanted."

"Why?"

"I don't know. Want to turn around and find out?"

I have to shout to be heard over the choppers that are hovering above the van. "Not a chance! Let's find a lightway and get the hell out of here!"

"I'm sorry."

"For what?"

"You could have been cured."

"That wasn't going to happen. I realize that now. You know what *will* happen though?"

"What?"

"We will save Mom," I tell her.

*Oh, how I love when Beth smiles.*

The van skids to a stop and the back doors fly open. We jump out, our hair whipping across our faces in the strong updraft from the two circling choppers. Three police vehicles are blocking the road. Galani, and a couple of police officers have given chase.

We run across the street onto a property with four greenhouses and duck between two of them. Two drones are buzzing closely behind us, no doubt transmitting images back to someone.

We ignore Galani's orders to stop. Beth lifts a chunk of concrete from a wheelbarrow and hurls it at one of the drones. The drone's movement is suspended and sparks fly as the second drone collides with it. They hover in a circle like dizzy bees for a couple of seconds, and then crash to the ground.

Galani and the cops are gaining on us. We blur past the greenhouses to an empty field overgrown with weeds. Our footsteps crunch across the frosted terrain. It's difficult to run and not trip on weeds, especially with the choppers directly above. It's hard to breathe from the cold wind they're stirring up, and I'm tiring. A third chopper is coming straight at us.

"You are surrounded." A man's voice projects from a loudspeaker. "Turn yourselves in. We mean no harm."

He is right about one thing. We are surrounded. Galani will catch up shortly, and the chopper in front of us is only a block away. So close to where our house would be in our world. While wondering how much farther I can run, a sliver of light flashes just ahead.

*The lightway!*

"Look, Syn!"

"I see it!"

"C'mon girls!" Galani shouts. "There's nowhere to run!"

*Wanna bet?*

We run, using every ounce of stamina we have left. Two new drones are buzzing alongside us as we near the edge of the field. They have to pull back when we squeeze through a narrow gap between two greenhouses. I run as fast as possible, despite my exhaustion.

We exit the narrow glass alley and halt in our tracks at the end of the property behind "ours." Two choppers are blocking our path.

*Dammit. We're so close!*

Galani and the officers are right behind us. "We don't want to hurt you."

"What was Jasper Inc. going to do with us once you handed us over?" Beth shouts.

Galani is clearly surprised that Beth knows about this. She doesn't answer.

"How about we make a deal?" I ask, turning to face them.

Galani laughs. "You're not in a position to bargain."

"If you're going to hand us over to a corporation for them to do who knows what to us, we have no incentive to tell you a thing. But if you allow us to return to our world, we'll take you to the portal."

The officers have no idea what I'm talking about. Galani dismisses the choppers with a wave. "Show me the portal!" She motions to the officers. "If they pull anything funny, shoot the kid."

"No way. She's no older than my daughter."

"That's an order!" Galani displays her true colors. "National Security trumps your conscience."

What Galani doesn't know is that only Beth and I can see or enter the portal. Otherwise, the chopper would have gone through it. She also isn't aware that we have played this game before, at gunpoint, and we escaped. Hopefully, this time makes us two for two.

Galani and the officers follow us through "our property". Unlike the surrounding lands, this is like the world we live in except that the garden has been let go. Litter is strewn about and the grass is covered with decomposing leaves. It's sad to see my oasis in this state.

We trudge through the garden and past the pond. It is covered with algae and bits of algae-coated trash are floating on the surface. The house looks far worse for wear than the garden. It is surely abandoned.

The lightway is only five feet away. Galani presses her gun against Beth's back. "How much farther?"

I hate myself for wanting to kill this woman.

"Almost there." Beth takes my hand.

The last time we escaped through a lightway at gunpoint, it was as our alt-dad shot at us, and we watched a bullet flying at us in slow motion. When we enter the lightway this time, we're not looking back. My world slows and I hope to god that Galani hasn't had time to shoot. When the light dissipates, my sister is right beside me, safe and sound.

"That seemed too easy."

"We're not done yet," Beth says.

It's for certain we have moved to another world. The air is frosty. I rub my arms briskly, trying to warm up. The garden we've landed in is well-manicured. Nearby, the sound of children laughing is music to my ears.

I follow Beth around the side of the house to where the children's voices are coming from. There we find a play structure featuring two swings, monkey bars, and a climbing wall that leads to a metal slide. A young boy and girl are being pushed on the swings by a middle-aged man I don't recognize. They are bundled up for the cold.

He seems glad to see me. "Are you the babysitter?"

"No," I tell him. "We, um…we thought this was Mr. Anderson's property."

"He's just down the road."

"Push us," the girl playfully chirps.

"Push us," the boy echoes.

"Your daddy is pushing you now. Are you having fun?"

"Yeah!" they chorus.

"Thanks for the directions," Beth calls as she follows me around the corner of the house.

I stop short, nearly colliding with a woman dressed in a gown for an evening out. Her hair is swept into a tidy low bun and her glasses are fogged up.

"I'm sorry."

"That's okay." She takes off her glasses to study me. "Are you Sandy?"

I'm about to tell her that I'm not the babysitter and am shocked with instant recognition. *Aunt Ruth!*

Not Masie Winters pretending to be Aunt Ruth, though the similarity is uncanny. No, I am facing an alternate version of my *real* aunt!

Chapter 31

# THE BURDEN OF RUTH

RUTH LOWERY BREEZES PAST ME. "Honey, the babysitter's here. Come and get ready. We're going to be late."

"She isn't the babysitter. They're looking for Joel's house."

"It's just down the road."

"Just down the road!" the little boy shouts. He squirms off the swing and runs to his mother.

Beth tugs my arm, but I don't budge.

"Is this your house?"

"Yes." She checks her watch, concerned that the babysitter is late.

"Mom, I wanna go inside," whines the little boy.

My curiosity is growing. "Did you inherit it?"

"Syn." Beth tugs my arm again.

"I did, as a matter of fact." She is scrutinizing me now, forgetting all about the babysitter and the son who is clutching her gown. "Who are you?

"Do you have any siblings?" Beth asks, hoping to move this along.

"I have a sister out East. Who are you and why are you asking so many questions?"

"I'm so sorry, Mrs. Eccleston!" A teenage girl rushes around the corner of the house and past the swings.

"Sandy's here!" squeals the little girl. She tries to climb off the swing and falls.

"Hey, Kiddo!" Sandy runs to help Mr. Eccleston with the shrieking child, followed by a concerned Mrs. Eccleston.

The Sandy Lopez of my world was in a couple of classes with me last year. This Sandy doesn't seem to know me at all.

Beth tugs my arm for the third time. This time, I let her pull me away while Sandy comforts the girl and the Ecclestons head inside their—our—house.

Beth leads the way while I'm deep in thought. After a few minutes, she stops and waits for me to catch up.

"Are you okay, Syn?"

"I'm fine. It's just that in this world Ruth got married and had kids. Those two little kids are like...our cousins." I clear my throat from emotion more than congestion.

*I should have pushed them on the swings.*

"In our world Ruth's life was cut short. She might have remained a single librarian for the next thirty years or she might have gotten married and had a family. It was her life to live as she wanted, and she never got the chance."

"It's cold. Let's keep going," says Beth. "We have to find the lightway."

We eventually end up at the Andersons' property and what we find there isn't surprising—an exotic animal refuge. Just like back home, Joel and Maggie Anderson are caring for reptiles that people realized were not cuddly pets, like a dog or a cat.

"I only knew Aunt Ruth—Masie—for six months." Beth dives into my thoughts. "She took really good care of you and took me in without any reservations. But now we know that she was a bad person."

"A bad person who ended up doing good things. She turned over a new leaf."

"She did, and it's okay to love her. She loved you and died for you."

"I'll always love her. But after seeing who my real Aunt Ruth was, what the woman who raised me did has become more…"

"Real?"

"She was a murderer. I will never forget. That would be a disservice to the memory of our real Aunt Ruth."

"Syn, it doesn't make you a bad person if you love her."

"I don't think it's possible for me to not love her."

"That's okay…. Are you cold? 'Cause I'm cold."

"Freezing."

I don't tell Beth that my chest is more congested than it was when I left the hospital, knowing it's only going to get worse.

While we're on the Anderson's property, we decide to look around before continuing to look for the lightway. The Joel and Maggie Anderson of my world stored a collection of tranquilizer guns that were used to knock out dangerous animals. Strong enough to put a gator to sleep.

"We should have some weapons on us when we return to the Garden."

"You mean…steal?" Beth grins.

"I learned from the best."

Beth's eyes twinkle and she punches me in the arm. "The driveway is empty and the lights are off in the house. I'll keep a lookout while you search the shed."

The shed is unlocked. I leave the door open for light because the bulb is burnt out. Luckily, the guns are right where they should be and I don't have to waste time looking. Even with Beth in sight just a few feet away, it's creepy sneaking around the dimly lit shed. I choose two dart guns and scrounge around until I have collected a dozen darts.

"Syn, someone's coming!"

*Oh crap!* I stuff everything into a backpack and peek out the door. The Andersons are driving up the road in their old pickup. I wait until trees are blocking their view and scoot from the shed to Beth's side.

Mr. Anderson stops the truck in front of us. "Are you young ladies lost?"

"Would you like to buy some Girl Guide cookies?" Beth asks, nonchalantly.

*Oh, Beth.*

"Oh good! Honey, get a couple of boxes," says Mrs. Anderson. "I forgot to pick up dessert."

"Um…Syn?"

The joke is on Beth now. I roll with it though, feeling pretty proud of my ingenuity. I unzip the backpack, hoping they don't recognize it as theirs, and rummage around, suddenly frowning. "Oh, I'm so sorry. We must have sold the last box to the Ecclestons."

"That's ok. We'll make popcorn," says Mrs. Anderson.

Mr. Anderson tips his hat to us and we trot off down the driveway.

"You're a genius!" says Beth.

I grin, wrapping my arms around myself in a failed attempt to keep warm. "I should have snuck into their house to get us some jackets."

"Can you say crime spree?" Beth laughs.

I realize how I'm normalizing theft, which is something I thought was abhorrent before learning that Beth was stealing to survive. Now it seems like a regular way of life when traveling through other worlds.

Soon we're both hungry. There is still no sign of the lightway and I'm coughing way more than I would like Beth to see. We check for unlocked doors on the cars we pass. A quick search in a pickup truck scores us a half-empty bottle of water and two sweaters.

*Win!*

A little farther down the road, Beth snatches some granola bars and a fruit leather from a minivan. I swipe a travel mug from the passenger seat and unscrew the lid. Old coffee.

Beth turns up her nose while I pour the gross brown liquid onto the grass. "There's a hose on the side of that house. We can rinse the mug there and fill it with water."

While I wait, plastered to the side of the old Tudor-style house, Beth sneaks over to the tap and unscrews the garden hose. Luckily, they haven't shut off the water yet for the winter season. She rinses the travel mug and fills it with fresh water.

As Beth quenches her thirst, I'm startled when a shadow blankets me. The shadow belongs to a man with a Santa-length white and grey beard.

"Can I help you?" he says.

"Oh, um…"

"Have you seen our cat?" Beth to the rescue again.

He narrows his eyes. "You girls live around here?"

Beth hands me the mug. "We're staying with my cousins for a few days. The Ecclestons."

*Smart girl.*

"Aw, Dave's family. Sorry, I haven't seen any cat. Go ahead and search the property. The farm is muddy though. Lots of rotten pumpkins too."

"Thanks. We'll be careful."

I gulp some water and pass it back to Beth. She drains what's left and leaves the mug beside the house.

The man has guests, but since we have his permission we aren't concerned about snooping around. The lightway is nowhere on his property though.

Beth sighs. "We're gonna have to snoop on the next property."

"At least we have a good excuse, thanks to you."

She pats her shoulder coyly.

The man waves from his window.

"Fluffy!" I call out.

"Kitty, kitty, kitty!" Beth climbs onto the wooden fence. "Here Fluffy!"

"Here lightway." I say, following Beth over the wooden fence.

"It must have heard you," says Beth. "Look!"

Sure enough, near the edge of the next field is the lightway. What a wonderful sight. Can I make it that far? It's getting increasingly harder to breathe.

I hand Beth a dart gun. With stolen guns tucked under stolen sweaters, we carefully make our way across the plastic tarp that's been laid over the crops to protect them from frost.

Beth laughs when a huge tabby cat streaks across our path. "There goes Fluffy!"

"Very funny."

"Bye bye, Fluffy," she sniffs, drawing her gun from beneath her sweater and heading into the lightway.

I'm right behind her, ready for the worst. When the light dissipates, we are in the Garden by the tree where Cole hanged Teng and Tian—to punish me.

From our position, the Garden is deserted and not at all like we left it.

# Chapter 32

# SINCE YOU'VE BEEN GONE

I'M RELIEVED TO BREATHE FREELY again, but it's impossible to ignore what has changed in the Garden.

Everything looks dull. The trees, grass, flowers—even Beth—are faded, like the color has been washed out of them. The scene reminds me of a TV show from the 50s.

The sky however, is anything but dull. It's red like a brilliant sunset. No, red like lava from a volcano, reminiscent of the sky in the apocalyptic world where I almost died on a graveyard of bones. That sky was blanketed with red fog.

The Garden is full of static electricity, although our hair isn't frizzy. Electricity sizzles in the air around us, zapping my hands. I jump with surprise from the harmless electric shocks. Wool fibers on my sweater are sticking out.

As we head for the bog, lightning flashes and thunder booms.

The air is warm, like when we left. Beth's cheeks are rosy.

The sweater is making me sweat. I strip it off and stuff it into the backpack, then wait for Beth to hand me hers.

"Make sure that no one is following us."

"The coast is clear," she announces, while I make room for her sweater in the now bulging pack. "It's eerie here with nobody else around."

Once we are on the path in the bog, I notice a blinking sliver of light nearby. It resembles a sheet of paper that's being held up to the light, with a tear in the center. The sliver of light has a very familiar pattern. It blinks three times, holds steady for twenty seconds and disappears, just like the lightways in the fog.

We cautiously move through the bog. When we reach the center where the muddy entrance to the sewers is located, I hear voices.

"Masies," whispers Beth.

We walk around the mud, pushing through ferns and a few prickly berry plants. I free Beth's sleeve from a thorn. When we see smoke and hear voices, we decide to hide behind some thick bushes.

In the middle of the field, not far from the spiral staircase, eight Masies are examining a small plane that has crashed. Smoke is billowing from the engine. The pilot's presumably dead body is draped over the partially open cockpit door.

*What the hell happened while we were gone?*

Another sliver of light flashes in the distance. One Masie approaches it cautiously, and tries to examine it while the final flash holds.

Beth motions for me to follow her and we retrace our steps, being extra careful that no one sees us. We spot Rose and Fawn and jog up to them with our fingers to our lips so they don't call out our names. They are happy to see us, but something is clearly bothering them.

I ask them to follow us into the fog.

"What the hell is going on?" I ask.

"We don't know," Rose says. "Nobody does."

"Those nasty clone women did this, that's for sure," Fawn adds. "Syn, have you seen Lily?"

"No. Why?"

"We can't find her anywhere."

"When did you last see her?"

"She was supposed to meet Lundy for dinner last night and never showed up. This is so not like her."

There is no static electricity in the fog, although the feeling of dread is making the hairs on my arm rise.

"Larry's missing too…since this morning." Rose looks around nervously. "I want to get out of here and make certain Flint is safe."

"Beth and I have to stay hidden," I call after them. "Please don't tell anyone you've seen us. We'll keep a lookout for Lily and Larry."

"Beth, something really bad is happening. We have no plan to rescue Mom and now we have to deal with missing people and a batty Garden."

"Lily and Larry probably went through a lightway. You saw the slivers of light. They may have entered by accident and will find their way back soon."

I hope she is right. Lily is my closest friend in the Garden, and Larry is the most warmhearted Creeper. I have always been fond of the lanky Ant-Man ever since we first met, when he was wearing grey sweats and a Nike sweatshirt. The memory makes me smile. I hope that nothing bad has happened to them.

Beth has her thinking cap on again. "We have to scope out the place and see what other weird stuff is going on, especially around the house where Mom is."

"Right."

"Then we recruit allies and come up with her rescue plan."

I hope the Masies still have use for Mom's brain. The alternative is something I don't even want to consider.

Once we reach the other side of the Garden, the band of fog thins somewhat. I poke my face through the border. We have a good view of the front of the house.

There is a strange chair on the lawn. It's wooden with a metal lining that runs up the legs and across the back, from which an assortment of wires protrudes. The wires stretch across the grass, up the front steps, and inside the front door.

One Masie is kneeling beside the chair, adjusting the metal lining attached to one of the arms. Lundy, looking truly miserable, is reluctantly running the wires between his fingers. Crouched next to Masie is none other than Synister.

I'm relieved that Synister is still alive, but Beth is furious.

"Why is she helping them?"

"Maybe she is being forced to help, like Lundy is."

Beth isn't listening because now she is gaping at the sky. Ominous clouds are blowing across it more rapidly than I have ever seen. The Garden is swiftly covered in darkness, the eerie red glow from the sky seeping through the clouds. A torrent of rain is unleashed.

Masie races to a blue tarp that's lying on the grass, with Synister hobbling behind her. Masie calls to Lundy and he rushes over with a hammer. He nails the tarp to the grass while Masie and Synister hold down the free edges. The downpour thunders onto the tarp, quickly forming puddles.

Masie and Synister trudge to the house, weighted down by their soaked clothing, screaming at Lundy to follow. He turns around briefly and holds up a finger to tell us to wait a minute.

*He knew we were watching!*

Beth and I are nice and dry in the fog when Lundy finally joins us.

"We didn't think you were coming," I say.

"Sorry. I couldn't sneak out right away."

"What's going on?" I ask.

"Things are getting really bad. They're forcing me to help them with this stupid chair contraption. I haven't seen Lily since yesterday, and they're keeping me so busy I can't even get away to look for her." He frowns. "Fawn and Nell are worried sick. I am too."

"Lily will turn up soon." I try to reassure him, and myself.

"Have you seen our mom?" Beth asks.

"She was in the house the whole time, but now she is…just…gone."

"Like…like the…others?" Beth stammers.

"The Stepford Clones say they have no idea where she is, but I don't buy it. They must have something to do with Lily's disappearance, and with Larry's. And I'm afraid, with your mom's."

I am terrified even thinking about what they could be planning.

# Chapter 33

# THE FATE OF A WORLD

ARE WE TOO LATE TO save Mom? Did something terrible happen to her, and to Lily and Larry?

"I have to get back before they get suspicious," Lundy says.

"Just tell us what happened while we were gone."

"Please." adds Beth.

"Okay. It's all just so crazy," he says. "After you left, they pulled that…disfigured…that…um…"

"Synister."

"They pulled Synister off your mom. She really has it in for her. Anyway, when Synister told them who she was and what your mom did to her in her world, they realized they had a common enemy."

I'm frustrated beyond measure. "So they're working together now. Great. Ya try to help someone…."

"After they brought Synister up to speed, she understood why your mom won't share her intel and told the Clone Club what they needed to know. Your mom's reaction confirmed it."

I was right. If Synister, of all people, knows what Mom has been holding back, it could only be one thing.…

"They took your mom into the Garden and no one has seen her since."

I let that sink in for a minute. "That chair outside…the one with the wires…it is meant for me?"

Lundy nods.

"They want to give themselves perfect health. Eternal life. To do for themselves what my parents wanted to do for me."

"Right. But in doing so—"

"They need me. The cure my parents were trying to create was focused on DNA. If they manage to perfect my parents' work…"

"Which they almost have," Lundy says.

"…then the healing properties will be transferred to my body. And just like the Synister I first met had unsuccessfully attempted to do, they will try to transfer the healing properties from me to each and every one of them."

"And the reason Mom won't tell them what they want to know," Beth starts.

"…is because I won't survive the process," I complete Beth's thought.

"Yeah, and get this," says Lundy. "They justify this madness because they believe that with eternal life, they will have an eternity to share their intellect with their prospective worlds, offering discoveries to humankind that may even save them from themselves. They think they are the good guys. Heroes."

"They're insane!"

"We won't let this happen," Beth says. "Their plan won't succeed without Syn. We could go find another world and never come back."

"The Masies have closed off all the lightways to other worlds. You're stuck here."

"Couldn't you set up a lightway so we all can get out of here? One that goes back to our home."

"They would kill him, Beth."

"I would do it if I could, cause if they capture you and their plan works, I'm dead too. But they changed the passwords and I have no access."

"Wait. Why would you be dead?"

"It's not just your life that would end, Syn. With their new healing properties, the Masies would transport to the Tether World and the Garden would cease to exist. Everyone here would die or just vanish. It would be like none of us ever existed."

This is a lot to take in.

Lundy ducks his head beyond the border of the fog and back. "I have to go."

"Can I ask one more question?"

"Yeah?"

"What is the Tether World?"

"The world the Garden is attached to, of course."

*What?*

Beth is equally clueless.

"The world it's attached to? But the Garden *is* a world."

"Oh, man. Your mom didn't tell you this? The Garden isn't a world of its own."

*Again…what?*

"Masie created the first Garden, not your parents."

*The first Garden being the valley where Roy and that terrifying monster reside.*

"But she couldn't create a new world that would contain the necessary properties to sustain life, like oxygen, gravity, water. You know, the important stuff. The Garden piggybacks off another world."

"The world whose sky we share," says Beth.

"Okay. So the water in the pipes and our electricity is all stolen from this Tether World?"

"And the airplanes? And the ones that crashed?" Beth asks.

"Yeah," Lundy says. "Plus, birds were dropping dead because your parents changed the climate to match a warmer part of the earth. They all came from this universe we're tethered with…the Tether World."

"But Lundy, that was ages ago. Even today, weird stuff is still happening."

"The Masies rebooted the Garden's attributes. It caused other damage too."

"That explains the red sky," Beth says. "And the dullness, and the sparks."

"Long story short, this isn't just about saving my life. It's about saving the lives of everyone in the Garden."

"Syn," Beth says, "the only way we can save everyone is to make sure you are safe."

"There is no way out of here. How long can Syn hide?"

"The voltway?" I ask. "Can we still—"

"Nope."

"Unless we guess their password," I say.

"I have a bot running. It's run through millions of combinations and so far no hits. These women are too smart to use the name of a pet or a simple phrase. I don't have much faith in figuring out the password."

"I gotta go. I've been gone too long already. Syn, listen to me." He looks me in the eyes. "Promise you won't let them find you. I know it sounds cliché, but the fate of this world rests on your shoulders."

*Totally cliché.*

"That is a lot of pressure."

"I know."

He is gone, leaving us in a long moment of heavy silence.

"That was a lot to take in," I say, mock-cheerfully, trying to release the pressure.

"Yeah." Beth says, totally serious.

"What if we head to the valley?"

"Syn..."

"I know, I know. That giant thing that wanted to eat us would love that. Roy has lived there for years though, and still has all his limbs intact."

"It will take a week to walk there. We don't have enough food and water."

"We stock up on food that's stored in the sewers."

"They will be there, waiting."

"We have dart guns. We get in, we get out. Then head to the test site Masie Winters created."

Beth sighs. "They will look for us there. They might even hurt Roy to get to us."

She's right. "So we'll hide out in the fog indefinitely. You have any other ideas?"

"What about the slivers of light?"

"Of course! They share the same pattern as the lightways."

"They have to lead somewhere. I'm guessing they're a path to—"

"The Tether World!"

Beth nods. "But we don't know where or when they will appear and we can't run around looking for them without being seen."

"We'd have to hide in the Garden and when we spot a sliver of light, run like hell, hoping we aren't caught."

"There's nothing stopping the Masies from following us there."

"No. But we'd have an entire world to hide in. Maybe we could even find help."

*And come back to rescue Mom.*

There is silence as we ponder the possibilities. I wonder if Beth is thinking what I'm thinking. She is after all, my fearless little sister.

I eventually break the silence. "We should go to this Tether World. It's our only chance—the Garden's only chance."

"And Mom's," she adds.

I have to hug her.

"If we bump into trouble," Beth's voice is muffled by my hair, "I'll distract them so you can save yourself."

I hold her at arm's length. "You really think I'd leave my sister behind?"

"If you get caught, I die anyway. We all do."

Beth is my Achilles' heel and she knows it.

"Okay, let's get moving. We shouldn't stay in one spot for—"

Beth reaches for my hand. "What's happening?"

The fog is growing darker, as if a monstrous storm cloud is drifting across the sun. Beth's face vanishes. It's pitch-black and I can't see a thing, until light reflects down on us.

Beth gasps. There's an image in the sky just like last time, when Mom projected her face above everyone in the Garden. Except that this time the image is anything but the face of a loved one, or a savior.

The giant face looming over us and the eyes that pierce through me belong to none other than Masie Winters.

# Chapter 34

# THE FACE OF FEAR

BETH'S WORRIES ARE TRANSMITTING THROUGH her hand, compounding mine tenfold. She is supposed to be the fearless one.

"Hello, Gardeners."

*I hate that smug face.*

"Let me remind you that we still mean you no harm."

*Bullshit.*

"We came to the Garden with a purpose, and for that we required the cooperation of Debra Wade. Unfortunately, she has refused."

"And that surprises you?" Beth sneers at the image in the sky.

"And now, the Garden—your home—is on the verge of catastrophe. You know what I'm talking about. You've seen it. You can feel it. The core of your peaceful oasis is shattering. However, we know what Debra Wade has been holding back. We have the piece of the puzzle that can stop the danger that looms over your home. We know how to get what we came here for. The final piece of the puzzle that can end this madness is an outsider. Her name is Synthia Wade."

As my name echoes around us, the dread that has encompassed me transforms into something else.

Anger.

"We have two requests: one for the people and creatures of the Garden, and one for Synthia herself. Synthia, if you care about the Garden and its residents, don't make us come after you. Somebody will get hurt. We are here in great numbers, so you can easily find one of us anywhere in the Garden."

*Not going to happen.*

She laughs. "But who am I kidding, right Syn? Of course you won't come forward. You and the members of the Wade family are selfish human beings who put themselves before everyone else.

"Friends of Synthia, you can't deny all the pain and suffering she has brought to your little paradise. Even still, you will not hand over your friend because we tell you it will save your world. You don't trust us, and why would you? Therefore, you require motivation. Synthia Wade requires motivation.

"To all the residents of this crumbling world, I ask you to find Synthia Wade. Bring her to us unharmed. Or bring us Bethany. When one sister is in trouble, the other will follow."

I instinctively try to make a fist but realize I'm squeezing Beth's hand.

"It's up to you all. But know this for sure: if Synthia Wade does not turn herself in within the next ten minutes, she will lose her mother."

The camera pans to a close-up of Mom's face. A strip of duct tape is covering her mouth, pure rage is smoldering in her eyes.

"No!" I'm still squeezing Beth's hand.

The sky projection pans out to show that Mom is on top of the staircase platform high in the sky.

"No, no, no," Beth mumbles.

"Every hour that we must wait for either Synthia or Bethany Wade, another member of your community will be thrown to their permanent death. To show you that we mean what we say, one of Synthia's friends is going to sacrifice her life."

*No, no, no.*

I expect the camera to show Rose's terrified face, but remember who else went missing, besides Mom…Larry and…

*Oh no.*

I'm engulfed with terror, cringing as two Masies appear on camera, dragging Lily to the railing. Duct tape is unceremoniously torn from her mouth. She struggles against her captors as they push her closer to the railing. There is no audio, so her screams are muted. Just the same, they pierce through my being, thanks to my sorry imagination.

I can only watch, dumbfounded and completely helpless, as they lift Lily's wriggling body and hurl my terrified friend over the railing.

# Chapter 35

# HELPLESS

IT SEEMS AS IF LILY'S body is falling through the sky right above me. Whatever lens is filming this is panning along with my friend as she falls, her blonde hair blowing through the air like the locks have a life of their own.

When I jumped off that platform I had help from a Creeper bird. Please let one of them swoop beneath her now. That would not save her though. I jumped of my own accord, and landed on the Creeper bird's back like it was a horse. Lily is in freefall and would simply bounce off from impact.

Silent tears are streaming down my cheeks. Beth is sobbing into my chest, unable to watch the projection any longer. My legs feel weak.

*Please don't let me faint.*

I remember the moment when Rose first introduced me to Lily, and how I was instantly drawn to her warm, genuine smile. Lily handed me a freshly picked apple and giggled when I said I didn't have money to pay for it.

When I was first trapped in the Garden, before I understood what this place was, I felt alone and afraid. Lily convinced me that everything would be okay. Her words and kindness brought comfort. I trusted her and decided that I had made a new friend for life.

Lily has been as good a friend to me in the Garden as Ebby and Jon have been back home. Like family. But, I know better than anyone that family can be taken away without notice. How this scene ends is not how I want to remember my friend. I stifle a sob, unable to watch Lily crash to the ground and break her neck. I at least will not allow Masie the satisfaction.

A broken neck is an immediate death and an immediate death in the Garden is a permanent death. The healing properties will not bring her back.

Lily is gone. My friend is deceased.

I hug Beth, wishing to never let her go. Two thoughts have consumed me—I hate myself for one of them. First, immense loss and sadness. Second, torment taints the gratitude I feel about Lily's death—gratitude that it wasn't someone else.

*Thank god it wasn't Beth.*

# Chapter 36

# NO TIME FOR TEARS

I FINALLY DARE TO LOOK up. Lundy has dropped to his knees and is cradling Lily's lifeless body, weeping.

*He really loved her.*

"It's time to plan our next move."

The voice in my ear is faint. I'm unable to respond to Beth, in shock from sadness and rage.

*I'll kill them all.*

Except for recent events, it's rare that I have ever wished death on anyone. But at this moment, I want to see Masie Winters—every last one of them—dead. They killed Aunt Ruth. They killed my friend. They…

*Mom!*

Just as I remember that her death was promised next if I didn't cooperate, the projection of Lily and Lundy is replaced with the evil face of Masie Winters.

"It troubled us to kill a young woman with so much promise. She had a long future ahead of her. Our thoughts are with you."

*Bullshit.*

"Now, back to business," she says cavalierly. "Synthia Wade, turn yourself in or your mother will share the same fate."

The fog lightens as the projection begins to fade. "I will be back for your mother's freefall debut in nine minutes and twenty-eight seconds, and counting."

I peer into Beth's teary eyes through my own tears.

"You can't do it, Syn. If she gets you, everyone dies. Not just you, everyone. Lundy, Rose, Mom. Me."

"There is only one way to save Mom, and everyone else," I say. "There is no other choice."

"We have to go," Beth agrees. "Now."

And hope that we can slip through one of those slivers of light to the Tether World…if they are lightways…without being caught. We have to make certain they see us leave the Garden. Their motivation for killing her is me turning myself in. And if I'm gone…

We both realize it's wishful thinking that they won't punish us for leaving and kill Mom anyway. But we don't have any other choice. There isn't enough time to recruit allies. Besides, they might turn us in and try to save themselves. People do desperate things when their lives are on the line.

"Let's go," I say.

Beth knows her way around the Garden better than anyone, so I trust her to lead me to the right place.

We dart through the fog, barely avoiding a collision with the occasional tree. My stomach is twisted in knots and my heart is pounding. What if those slivers of light don't lead anywhere?

*How much time is left?*

As if on cue, Masie's voice echoes throughout the Garden. "Five minutes remaining, Synthia. Your mother's time is running out. Now that your friends can see how you are not as heroic as you make yourself out to be, and how selfish you are to let your own mother die, you won't be running for much longer."

"Almost there," Beth says.

*We're cutting it close.*

"So, my Garden friends," Masie continues. "Catch Synthia or her sister. Bring one of them to us and save not only the life of Debra Wade but the lives of your friends and family. Save yourselves."

"After we exit the fog we should be at the entrance to the bog," Beth says.

"There will likely be Masies waiting for us."

"We each have six darts. Only shoot if we get split up or I run out."

"Okay."

"Let's stay together. As soon as a sliver appears, sprint to it."

*And hope it takes us somewhere.*

"Okay, Sis. Let's go!"

We leap past the fog barrier into the Garden. Sparks illuminate the air, each for a split second at a time.

"There they are!"

"Okay, they see us!"

We race ahead. Mom can't have more than three minutes left.

There is distinct shuffling around us as throngs of Masies…*and maybe friends*…take pursuit. The spiral staircase comes into view on our left. It's tempting to race up the stairs and rescue Mom, but that would be doomsday for the Garden. In the orchard ahead of us, a sliver of light flashes. We make a mad dash.

"Get them!"

Shuffling sounds follow closely as we zigzag through the orchard, not daring to look back. My knees buckle with the realization that we have just run by the spot where Lily's body is resting.

"Keep going! We can do this, Syn!"

The sliver of light blinks, flashes, and flashes again. We should be able to make the final flash because it holds for twenty seconds.

I'm suddenly pushed and roll to the ground. I shoot a dart into the figure looming over me and roll out of the way before the sleepy Masie falls.

Beth is struggling with two Masies. She manages to shoot them both and get to me before they hit the ground. More shadowy figures have surrounded us.

"We gotta go!"

*We're going to miss the opening!*

Masie's face appears in the sky, darkening our world again. "You just signed your mother's death warrant."

The projection in the sky zooms in on Mom. She is being lifted into the air. There is terror on her face, but she is not fighting like Lily was. Mom is flung over the railing.

My world is spinning. I can't breathe. "No!" I fall to my knees.

Someone pulls me up. It's Butterfly-Man. Rat-Girl is carrying Beth, who is desperately trying to squirm free.

"You got them!" shouts one Masie.

"Good job!" squeals another.

I am surprised when Butterfly-Man and Rat-Girl start racing for the orchard. They're not turning us in, they're helping us!

The sliver of light is not blinking. There is no telling how long it has been holding steady. It could blink off at any second!

"If you're smart," Butterfly-Man says, "you won't return!"

He shoves us both into the light.

The last thing I see is Mom, falling to her death.

# Chapter 37

# THE TETHER WORLD

TIME DOESN'T FREEZE AS IT does in a regular lightway. Instead, the tragic event of our mother freefalling to her death is chopped up like an animated Picasso painting, followed by glimpses of a field in daylight intertwining with a dark Garden. Within a few seconds, the field becomes the most prominent image. Before I know it, all the pieces are in place, as are we.

We are in a field a few properties over from ours. Most of the weird changes in the Garden—the red sky, sparks in the air, and the dull colors are shared by this world, though so far, there are no slivers of light like the one we just came through.

"We are most definitely in the Tether World," says Beth.

"Thanks to our Creeper friends!"

I'm suddenly not feeling so good. I bend over and throw up. Beside me, Beth is doing the same.

"Mom." I spit out the last of it.

"We have to keep moving." Beth wipes her mouth. "The Masies *will* follow."

In other words, there is no time to mourn.

As we run to the road, my thoughts are so focused on Mom it doesn't immediately register that mucus is beginning to clog my lungs. All I can think about is Mom falling to her end, helpless. Not only because there is no way to save herself, but because she doesn't know if her children will survive. After everything she has sacrificed to protect us, she will never know whether or not her efforts were in vain.

I stop running, unable to ignore my condition any longer. While coughing for a good long minute, tears of grief are streaming from my eyes.

"We're orphans," I finally manage to say.

Beth and I hold each other for a long time, lost in grief.

"Syn," Beth says, wiping her tears, "we still have each other. And we owe it to Mom to take care of ourselves. Let's lose ourselves in the city. Someplace public where the Masies will have a hard time finding us."

"I need to go to the hospital," I confess.

When the treatment they gave me in that *Futurama* World wears off, I will be in a terrible state, not having taken medicine or performed treatments for a month.

"Of course. We'll need to 'borrow' a car."

We head down the road, searching for a car to drive to the city. The road is similar to the one back home except that the pavement is cracked as if from an earthquake. The sky is red and the colors dull. It's warm for late November, the temperature here the same as it was in the Garden.

We walk past our house in this world. It's identical to the one back home, aside from the chipped paint. There is no vehicle parked in the carport or driveway.

An SUV drives past. The driver doesn't notice us, but we sure notice her.

*Masie!*

Not just any Masie either. Her hair is tied back and she's wearing glasses like Aunt Ruth. She pulls into the driveway, signaling first like Aunt Ruth always did, whether or not there was another car in the vicinity.

"Let's go back to *our house*," I say.

"Bad idea. That's the first place they'll look."

"I have an idea. It's crazy, but maybe…"

Beth sees my determination. She nods her reluctant approval.

A minute later, I'm walking up the driveway. Masie—*Ruth Lowery* in this world—has just opened the trunk. She reaches for the strap of a grocery bag.

"Masie."

*I should have called her Aunt Ruth.*

"Oh, Syn, would you—" Ruth freezes when she turns around and sees us standing on the driveway behind her. She glances from one of us to the other. "I knew this day would arrive. You shouldn't have come here."

Ruth pulls a handgun from a side holster hidden under her shirt. She aims the gun in Beth's direction and pulls the trigger, then towards me and shoots again.

## Chapter 38

# A WHOLE NEW WORLD

THERE'S A THUD BEHIND ME, and another.

*We're still alive!*

On the driveway behind us lie two Masies, blood seeping through a hole in the center of their foreheads.

Ruth rifles through a blue plastic bin in the carport, producing an orange tarp. She covers both bodies with it, and then puts a large rock on each corner.

"Get inside," she orders, slamming the trunk with the groceries still inside. "Hurry!"

We follow Ruth up the familiar concrete stairs to the front door. She checks for any more signs of trouble and motions for us to come inside.

"Stay here for a minute." She leaves us in the entrance hall and goes outside, leaving the front door ajar.

Curious, I peek into the kitchen, and gasp.

*I'm* in the kitchen. Not me, *another me!* She is sitting on some guy's lap, making out with him. I recognize the guy. He is the same blonde-haired boy from one of the visions I had while falling through the Oblivion.

*Kissing a tall blonde boy at the beach. A boy I've never seen in my life?!*

The vision of the women stalking my house turned real. It was a preview into my future. At some point will I be making out with this boy, perhaps back home in my world? Or was that vision a preview of *this* Syn's life?

The boy opens his eyes and spots me. Startled, he jumps up, almost knocking the other Syn to the floor.

"What's wrong?" She turns around to see what her boyfriend is gaping at. "What the…?"

"I told you to stay in the hall!" Ruth snaps, brushing past us.

"Masie!" The other Syn is panicked. "What's going on?"

*Masie? The other Syn knows who she really is!*

"Zach, you have to leave."

The boy's jaw is hanging wide open. His eyes are fixated on me.

"Now!"

Zach ambles to the front door, his eyes still on me, and then remembers his girlfriend.

"And Zach?" Ruth says.

"Uh, yeah?"

"Let's keep Syn's twin a secret."

"Uh, okay."

"No, not 'uh okay'. Zach. It. Does. Not. Leave. This. House. Understood?"

His Syn nods, telling him it's okay. Ruth locks the front door behind Zach and goes into the closet for a moment. She reappears wearing a medical face mask and hands one to me and to the other Syn. "Put these on."

The other Syn puts on her mask. "Is she…one of them?"

"This is Synthia Wade from Earth 03241944," Ruth says.

*Earth 03241944?*

"And her sister, I presume?" Ruth asks.

I nod.

The other Syn gazes at Beth. "I have…a sister?"

Beth waves. "Hi."

My chest has grown more congested and I have to cough again. Ruth hands me a glass of water, which I gulp down.

"We all have questions…but we aren't safe, are we?" Ruth asks, just as the doorknob on the back door rattles.

"We're not."

The other Syn peers through the kitchen window and jumps back like she has seen a ghost. "It…it's you…another Masie!"

BANG!

Masie is trying to kick in the door. Ruth looks through the peephole, draws her gun, and pulls the trigger. The other Syn's piercing scream is followed by a heavy thud outside. Ruth opens the door to a dead Masie, crumpled on the stairs.

"What the hell?!" the other Syn screams, then coughs into her arm. "Is she dead?"

This craziness must all be new to her. Or is it? She's aware of Ruth's true identity and knows about other worlds, so she is not totally in the dark.

Ruth dashes into the living room and returns with a laptop. "Kids," she says, sitting down at the kitchen table and turning on her computer, "keep watch and tell me when you see any more of them."

Beth drags a chair to the entrance hall and climbs onto it so she can see through the peephole. I stand apart from the other Syn at the kitchen window. Occasionally, we glance at each other, awkwardly.

"I'm sorry to bring this to your home," I tell her, idly watching a bird fly past.

"What is *this?*" she asks.

I spot four more Masies approaching the property next door and point them out to the other Syn.

"Oh," she says. "Masie, there are more of…uh… *you* coming."

"Four of them," I add. "A minute away at the most."

Ruth keeps her eyes trained on her laptop. "Alright." She's frantically typing who-knows-what on the keyboard. "Get your sister. I'm almost ready."

"Ready for what?" the other Syn asks.

I check out Ruth's computer screen as I return from the entrance hall with Beth. She's using some sort of coding program, like what Mom and Lundy used in the Garden.

The top of a Masie's head passes by the kitchen window.

"They're here!" the other Syn shouts.

"Alright. Each of you hold onto something that is attached firmly to the floor."

The other Syn and I take hold of the windowsill. Beth clutches a cupboard handle and the counter. Ruth remains seated at the table.

One Masie spots us through the window and darts for the porch stairs. She takes the first step and the entire house shakes like there's a small earthquake. She falls into the arms of another Masie. They both try again, with two more Masies close behind. The knob on the back door starts to rattle and then—

BOOM!

There's a flash of light and the house jolts like a truck hit it.

Ruth raises her handgun, opens the door, and shoots the first two Masies squarely in the chest. Before they even hit the ground, she hops over the dead body of the first kill and shoots the remaining Masies. Then she sprints back inside and locks the door.

"We're safe now."

"We're not safe," Beth says. "They'll keep coming."

"No, they won't. This house, with us in it, just jumped into another world. They won't find us."

"Wait, what?" the other Syn shouts. "We're in another world? How? What is happening here?"

The other Syn and I start coughing simultaneously like we really are one and the same.

Ruth opens a cupboard, identical to the one my aunt installed when she had our kitchen renovated. She takes out a glass and picks up the one I already used, fills them both with water from a tap on the fridge and hands them to me and the other Syn.

I remove my mask and gulp down the entire glass, and cough, cough, cough.

"Syn," Ruth says to her Syn. "Please go upstairs and bring down your extra nebulizer, your vest, and anything else that our guest here can use."

The other Syn stares at her guardian with frustration and disbelief.

"I'll explain everything later. Now, please go."

She shakes her head, but obeys.

When she's out of earshot, Ruth turns to us. "Let's have a little chat."

Chapter 39

# SECRETS AND LIES

I BEGIN WITH MY PARENT'S disappearance, giving Ruth the *CliffsNotes* version of everything we've been through.

The other Syn brings down the equipment and while Beth tells the rest of our story, I hook myself up to the therapy vest. The other Syn sits with us in the living room, in awe while Beth quickly moves through the sequence of events. The room grows silent when she pauses.

"What is it, Beth?" Ruth is concerned.

My sister can only gaze at the floor as she reveals the heartbreaking deaths of Lily and Mom. She raises her eyes to mine and I click off the vest, surrendering to another good cry.

"I'm so sorry," the other Syn says.

"As am I," Ruth says.

I cough up phlegm the vest has dislodged and dry my eyes.

Ruth kindly assists me in taking off the vest. "It sounds like the Ruth who raised you was similar to me in many ways."

"But here, I…Syn…knows who you are," I say. "And she doesn't seem to have a problem with it."

Ruth chuckles. "Oh, she took it hard when I first told her."

"You *told* her?" I'm surprised.

"Those planes that crash-landed in the Garden," Ruth says, "came from this world."

"I'm aware."

"The weather changes and airplanes disappearing in the same trajectory was a big thing," Ruth explains. "The story got worldwide media coverage. Changes in weather patterns affected the entire world, and have ever since. I was partly responsible for doing the same thing to another world when I created my test site. Syn had so many questions. And the effects of what I did weighed on me. So I told her the truth."

"I was furious," the other Syn says. "But then she tried to bring my parents back. And…well…they were dead. Killed by the one you call Synister."

"Oh," I say.

"It took a while," Ruth says. "But Syn and I grew close over time. We were all we had and we made it work. I can't change what I did or bring her parents back. But I spend every moment of my life doing my best to make up for it."

"My Aunt Ruth…Masie…did the same. Now she is gone, and our parents are gone. Beth and I are all alone."

"We have each other," Beth says.

"Always."

"I can't believe I have a sister," the other Syn says.

"So you know about…everything?" I ask her.

"Almost everything." She glances at Ruth. "How the hell did you jump our house into another world?"

*Good question.*

The garden I see through the living room window is an exact replica of the garden in the world we just came from.

"I won't bother explaining the complexities of the science. A stranger stopped by yesterday, so I knew this would happen soon. I didn't know that Syn and Beth would show up, just that my evil others would. So, I created a way for us to escape and hide from them for as long as possible."

Suddenly, something Ruth just said clicks and gives me a glimmer of hope. "You said you had a visitor yesterday. Who was it?"

"An interesting-looking fellow. He said his name was Larry."

*Yes!*

"He's fine," Ruth says after noticing my reaction. "He was obviously out of place, but I helped send him on his way back home."

I'm relieved that Larry wasn't sitting on top of the platform in the Garden, waiting to be thrown to his death.

"Did this house…smush the house that was here?" the other Syn asks.

"Of course not, Synthia," Ruth chuckles. "We swapped places with the house that was in this place. No one was living there, so it's fine."

"Why wasn't anyone living there?" I ask.

Ruth frowns. "One of my others came to kill the Wades in this world. They succeeded in killing just…their daughter."

*That world's Syn.*

"Her parents survived the attack. They fought back and the killer escaped to another world. I believe the heartbroken parents managed to follow her to this world, intent on killing her. A bullet was shot into an oil tanker and all three were killed in the explosion."

Beth and I exchange a knowing glance. That explosion was certainly in our world. That would explain why Masie's body and the charred bodies that were suspected to belong to our parents were discovered not long after their disappearance.

"So, you two. What is your plan? Would you like to stay with us tonight or do you have something else in mind?"

I wanted to come here purely so Ruth could protect us from any Masies that followed from the Garden. But there was no plan. Then I think about the ideas Beth and I have spun around, which might defeat our enemy. This Ruth might be able to help.

"The frequency," I say, "the one Synister initially used to attack the Creepers' senses and drive them underground, and that Cole later changed to affect humans? Is it possible to adjust that frequency to affect your others?"

Ruth considers this. "A frequency that affects a specific person rather than a species is complicated, but it is possible to adjust."

"Would you be able to return to the Garden with us and adjust the frequency to help defeat your others?"

"Whoa!" the other Syn yells. "I know you and I are the same and all that, but she is *my* family."

I don't blame her for feeling resentment. I would feel the same way. I mean, we are the same. Sort of.

"I know it's a big ask, but—"

"A big ask? You're asking my only family member to leave me and do something that will ultimately harm her."

"A good set of earplugs should protect me," Ruth says. "The problem is, even if the frequency can be adjusted to affect a specific person, it would take a lot of time to implement."

"Good," the other Syn says. "That is settled."

"That said," Ruth begins, "I have a couple of other ideas that might help you girls solve your problem."

"What problem?" asks the other Syn. "They are safely out of the Garden now. Without Syn there, those other Masies can't hatch their evil plan and the Garden is safe."

"That's what I thought when I left the garden with Beth. But since meeting you, something has been nagging at me. We may have only delayed the inevitable."

Beth frowns. She knows what I'm thinking.

"There are an infinite number of worlds in the multiverse," I say. "They can simply pluck another one of me from an alternate world and use her for their procedure."

The other Syn considers how another one of us will die if nothing is done. "Okay. But listen. The Masies search for you. Some are killed and you are nowhere to be found. They are probably *already* hopping through the multiverse to find another one of…*us*."

"Not yet," says Ruth. "We have a little time before they go down that route."

"Why is that?" I ask.

"I may be different than they are, but as much as I hate to admit it, we are the same person. We think the same way. They won't resort to using one of your others for the same reason they waited it out when you escaped to a series of other worlds. They killed people you cared about to get you to turn yourself in rather than kidnapping another Synthia Wade."

It clicks.

"Because no matter how much they claim they have moved on from revenge, the thought of killing the daughter of the Ian and Debra Wade who hurt them in the first place is just too sweet for them to ignore."

"Had they not needed you for their plan," Beth says, "they would have killed you—and probably me—anyway."

"You would do that?" the other Syn asks her guardian.

"I am capable of many evils, Syn. I did kill your actual aunt."

"I know, but…"

"No buts about it. I did terrible things. Your parents are dead partly because of me. I love you, so the person I am now could never harm you or any version of you. But the person I was twelve years ago absolutely could. I am trying to make amends every single day, and that is why I am going to do this."

"But you didn't start any of this. That other Masie Winters did. This isn't your battle."

"I lost my battle, Syn," Ruth says. "I never atoned for what I did."

"You have." A tear makes its way down her cheek. "You've been here for me."

"I always will be. I wouldn't get myself into any-thing that would keep me from returning to you. I can do this and still come back to you. One thing that's true about this cult-of-sorts is that they never harm their own."

"Still, you have already broken that rule," the other Syn says. "And you are planning on doing it again."

"The rule doesn't apply to me." Ruth smiles. "Thanks to you, I broke free from that cult long ago."

Watching Ruth and the other Syn hug is bitter-sweet. I will never hug my Aunt Ruth again.

"Syn and Beth, you will stay the night. I will work on a plan and if I can figure this out, we leave tomorrow morning."

* * *

Ruth's lasagna tastes exactly like the lasagna I first tasted at the age of five. This could be the last time I enjoy the taste of the peppery tomato sauce, tender pasta, and mushrooms that practically melt in my mouth.

After dinner, my chest is on fire and growing congested yet again. I insist I can survive the night without getting medical attention if Ruth and the other Syn help me with various treatments.

The other Syn lends us buttoned pajamas. While mine fit perfectly, Beth's do not. It looks like she is playing dress-up in grown-up clothes.

Beth and I gratefully flop on the living room couch while the other Syn helps Ruth with the dishes. So much has happened, but the loss of Lily and Mom has not left my mind. The sofa is comfortable and I sink into it, drawing Beth close. We enjoy the closeness for a while, sitting in silence, consoling each other.

The other Syn soon strolls in and takes a spot on the sofa beside Beth. I watch her take her mountain of pills, which I should be doing too.

"I'm really sorry about your mom and your friend," she says.

"Thank you," I say. "I'm sure you can relate better than anyone."

She is thoughtful. "Back in your world, did you have a friend named Janna?"

"I...I did. It shouldn't be a surprise to hear Janna's name, but it is. "She died a while back."

"My Janna died too."

While we share DNA, the other Syn and I are different in many ways. She's more open and transparent, not afraid to say what she feels. She is easily excitable and confrontational. Still, we share a common bond. We have shared the loss of our parents and friends, the struggle of fighting an incurable disease, and the betrayal of our guardian. And though Beth is my sister, I can sense the closeness she feels for the girl she only just met.

"Tell me about your friend," the other Syn asks. "Lily?"

Immediately, more tears pour out as if floodgates have just been lifted. She cries too. We cough into our masks in unison and it feels like I'm watching my reflection in a mirror. Beth snuggles into me, gently taking my hand.

* * *

I lie awake, thinking about our return to the Garden and what comes next if we're successful. I contemplate many things—one in particular—while Beth and the other Syn sleep. Finally, I find the courage to get out of bed and tiptoe down the hall to Ruth's room.

She is sitting at her desk, staring at her laptop screen. I tap lightly on the door and it swings open.

Ruth turns around. "Is everything okay?"

"Can I talk to you for a minute?"

"Of course."

I shut the door and wait to hear the click before speaking. Ruth sits down on the end of her bed and pats a spot beside her.

"What I suggested earlier," I cough and lean against the door for support, "about changing the frequency to—"

"It's a good idea. But I'm…"

"It's not that. It's something else I want you to do when you're in the Garden."

"And that is?"

I sit on the bed beside her to explain. It's difficult to get it all out between coughs, and to sound confident. But I manage to spill everything.

Ruth studies me for a few seconds. "Let me get you a drink of water." She leaves me on the edge of my seat, literally.

"Okay," she hands me a full glass. "Why would you want me to do that?"

I take a long drink, considering the best way to explain everything. I choose my words carefully and she listens intently. "So," with great anticipation, "would that be possible?"

"It's a much simpler task than the main objective."

"Of course, changing the frequency and saving the Garden is our priority. But could you do this as well?"

"I don't know, Syn." She toys with a loose thread on the bedspread. "You might regret this someday."

"It's very possible I will. That is why I'm asking you right now."

She studies me carefully, with much compassion. "I'll consider it. Now go to bed. Don't let this keep you up all night." She takes my empty water glass.

"Fair enough." I pause at the door. "One more thing."

"What's that?"

"Please keep this conversation between us."

"You mean..."

"Beth can never know."

## Chapter 40

# THE FOLLOWER

SOMETHING IS TICKLING MY CHEEK and I groggily open my eyes. It's 8:14 A.M. and a cat is licking my face. Not an alternate version of my ironically named hairless Sphinx, Fluffy, like I might expect. This cat has plenty of orange hair with a few streaks of black that give it character.

So as it seems, with the other Syn knowing that her Aunt Ruth is really Masie Winters, Ruth had no reason to fake an allergy to cats and insist on getting a hairless critter for a pet. I sit up, petting the cat that was purring before I even touched him.

The sound of muffled voices travels down the hallway. Beth's bed is empty. I put the cat down and it scurries under the bed, obviously just liking me for the attention.

Thankfully, chest congestion didn't stop me from sleeping, because today is going to be a long day. I amble to the washroom, almost tripping over the cat as he darts across the room. My concerned reflection greets me over the sink. A few painful coughs help clear my chest somewhat, but this decline of health is concerning.

The cat almost trips me again on my way downstairs. My reflexes are still good. I'll take that as a positive sign. The other Syn and Beth are chatting away in the kitchen, just like the two of us would be doing over breakfast. I'm glad they are getting along. When I stroll into the kitchen, the other Syn has just set a glass of milk on the table in front of Beth.

"Good morning," says Beth, wearing a fresh milk moustache.

The other Syn grins at me. "I guess that's what I look like after just getting out of bed. Good to know."

I chuckle, but that makes me cough. I take a seat beside Beth and reach for a piece of toast.

"You okay?" Beth asks.

"I'll live."

"I hope so." Ruth is leaning against the doorway, watching us.

Her hair is wet and she's wearing a white bathrobe so generic it could have been swiped from a hotel. She's holding a light green blouse and a pair of beige pants.

"Will I fit in wearing these, Syn?"

The other Syn is confused. "Fit in?"

"They're perfect. Your hair is a few inches too long though. Beth can fix that."

"Ooh, a makeover," says Ruth. "I'll need more caffeine first." She tosses the clothes on a chair and shuffles over to the coffee pot under the other Syn's suspicious eye.

"Hey…Syn," I change the subject quickly. "So, you have a boyfriend."

She blushes. Ruth chuckles and takes a sip of coffee. "Time for my exit." She heads upstairs to change.

"I'm outta here too," Beth groans. "No boy talk for me, thanks." She races up the stairs after Ruth.

"Yep, I have a boyfriend," she laughs. "What about you?"

"Not right now. I used to date someone, but now we're just good friends."

"What's his name? Maybe I dated him too."

"Jon Ladage."

"Jon Ladage?" The other Syn is floored. "Oh. My. God."

"I'm guessing you didn't go out with him?"

"Ha ha, no. But maybe he's cooler in your world."

*Jon is not cool, but he is pretty terrific.*

"Do you know Ebby Davis?" I ask.

"Yeah. We were best friends for a couple of years. But after her brother Luke was killed in Afghanistan, she kept to herself."

Luke died in this world. I let that sit with me for a moment. "I'm sorry to hear about your Luke," I say quietly.

"That's okay. It's nice to know that Luke is still alive in your world."

I give her some time to reminisce about her Luke, totally relating to how she must feel. She doesn't cry though, obviously having accepted that he's gone.

"So, back to that guy you were making out with yesterday. Zach's cute."

"You guys didn't date?"

"Never seen him before." There's no reason to mention that I saw him kissing her—*or me*—in a vision.

"He's great," the other Syn says. "When I was in the hospital a couple of months ago, he came every day after school to be there with me and catch me up with whatever was going on. He's super supportive and isn't freaked out by my CF."

"I hope our abrupt entrance yesterday didn't freak him out."

Her cheeks grow pink. "Just a little. I texted him last night to tell him I'd explain after our trip."

"What trip?" Ruth strolls into the kitchen, wearing a new hairdo and the drab outfit I approved earlier.

*Nice work, Beth.*

"You know... the Garden."

Ruth is determined. "You're not coming with us. It's too dangerous."

"If it's too dangerous, why are *you* going?"

"You already know why. If I have to worry about you, I'll be off my game. You'll be much safer here. End of discussion."

Ruth dismisses the other Syn's pleading eyes and unlocks the door to the basement. "Follow me, girls." She tugs the string to turn on the light, more firmly than necessary.

The other Syn groans and follows us down the stairs, mumbling something to herself that I can't make out.

The basement is being used for storage. Next to an old wooden rocking horse is a rack crammed with outdated clothing. Familiar toys are strewn about on shelves, and boxes are overflowing with old tools.

Ruth presses a hand against the wooden paneling and a rectangular section of wall creaks open, revealing a glass panel. She places one hand against the glass and a green light outlines her handprint. The green light fades and a lit number pad appears, upon which she types a four-digit code. Nothing happens.

"Well, that was anticlimactic," the other Syn jests.

"Just wait." Ruth holds up a hand.

Sure enough, she has set something in motion. A dragging sound has commenced from deep within the basement on the other side of the stairs. She leads us to where the wall has opened to reveal an unfamiliar section of the basement.

We are standing in a square room the size of an average bedroom. Metal cupboards line each wall. There is another keypad on the wall.

Again, Ruth keys in a four-digit code. Every metal cupboard door opens. One cabinet contains weapons.

I have chills from the sobering sight of guns, ammo, rifles, grenades, smoke bombs, and an assortment of sharp knives.

"Holy shit!" Beth and I say in unison.

The cupboards on one wall contain non-perishable food such as canned soup, crackers, and bottled water. The others contain tech. Except for some wires and a couple of tablets, I don't know what this stuff is for.

Ruth retrieves two metal discs from a top shelf, each about the size of a hockey puck. She wraps them in bubble wrap and slides them into a backpack, along with two water bottles and some granola bars. She hands the bag to me.

"Do you need this one too?" The other Syn hands Ruth another backpack.

"Thanks, Honey." Ruth tosses in four bottles of water and more granola bars.

Ruth is eyeballing the weapons now, finally deciding on a smoke bomb and two boxes of ammo. Into the bag they go. She checks to make certain the silver handgun isn't loaded and places it in the backpack.

"Beth, this bag is for you. Do either of you shoot?"

"Of course, they don't shoot," the other Syn says.

"Beth does," I blurt.

"What?"

Ruth hands a pistol to Beth. "How is this?"

"You just handed a gun to a child!"

"She's not just any child," I tell the other Syn.

"I'm not a child, period." Beth points to a silver handgun. "How about the nine-millimeter?"

"The nine-millimeter?" the other Syn exclaims.

Ruth takes back the pistol and hands Beth the silver handgun.

"Syn's becoming a pro with a tranq gun," Beth says.

"I wouldn't say I'm a pro."

"I don't have any tranquilizer guns." Ruth hands me the pistol Beth rejected. "Just in case."

"Are you going to start handing out WMDs like Halloween candy?" the other Syn quips.

"Not today."

* * *

After an emotional goodbye with the other Syn and a tender moment between her and Ruth, we begin our journey.

"We'll walk half a mile to be sure to enter the Garden in the fog, where we'll be hidden."

Ruth leads us deep into a cornfield and stops. She unzips my backpack and removes one of the metal discs. "Be aware that we might not land in your Garden, so be prepared for anything."

"What happens if it's not our Garden?" Beth asks.

"Then we find a rabbit hole."

"Rabbit hole?" I ask, gazing at Beth.

Beth shrugs.

"Where is this lightway anyway?" I ask, scanning across the tall stalks of corn.

"I'll lead the way," says Ruth. "Ready?"

"Ready."

Truth be told, I am terrified we might see Mom's lifeless body, not to mention any other terrible things that have happened in the Garden while we've been gone.

Ruth puts the disc on the soil, stomps on it, and jumps back. A lightway beams upwards from it.

"Right on," says Beth. "Into the lightway!"

The new world is a Garden, yet we don't know if it's our Garden. The lightway did land us in a foggy forest, however, which looks identical to the Garden I'm hoping we're in. It's a relief that my lungs have already begun to clear up. I would have been in very bad shape soon.

"Okay, our next step is…" Ruth pauses as footsteps approach.

All three of us swing around, guns raised. A figure appears in the fog and as it approaches, my grip on the gun tightens. Finally, the figure is in clear view.

"You!" Ruth shrieks with disbelief.

"Hey guys," the other Syn says.

# Chapter 41

# BEHIND ENEMY LINES

"WHAT ARE YOU DOING here?" Ruth shakes the other Syn by the shoulders.

"Oh, come on. You know I couldn't miss a chance to see the magical Garden I've heard so much about." She inhales deeply. "I'm healthy. For the first time in my life I feel great. Like, *really* great!"

"It's nice, isn't it?" I say quietly.

"I thought you understood how your being here would put this whole mission in jeopardy." Ruth is irate.

"I was going to follow you guys from behind. You weren't even supposed to see me."

"Great stealth work there," Beth quips. "You almost lasted for a whole minute."

"Syn and Beth, I'm afraid this changes things." Ruth glares at her Syn. "We have to go back."

"Like hell," the other Syn says. "You're not going back because of me."

"You should have thought about that before you disobeyed me."

"Don't let them down because of me. I won't leave! I'll run away and hide in the fog where you can't find me."

Nobody knows what else to say. Fog envelops us as if inviting our next move, but the mission is stalled. My cheeks are hot from the uncomfortable silence, so the cool mist is pleasing.

"Don't you want me to enjoy feeling healthy?" the other Syn breaks the silence.

Ruth throws up her hands in despair. "Fine! You will do exactly what I say. No second-guessing me."

"Aye aye, Captain." The other Syn triumphantly displays her backpack. "Extra water and protein bars."

"At least she came prepared," I say.

Beth rolls her eyes.

Ruth shakes her head and unfolds the map I sketched.

"So," I say, wanting to move this mission forward, "you're heading to the house?"

"Yes."

"You look like every Masie in the Garden," the other Syn says, "so this should be easy peasy."

*Like anything ever is.*

"You all wait here."

And with that, Ruth is gone.

Beth leans against me and takes the other Syn's hand. They've only known each other for one day and are already so connected, just like when I first met my sister.

Trying to keep busy, I rummage through my backpack and pull out a granola bar. Beth and the other Syn watch me unwrap it. Nobody wants to talk, so I chew, and chew. My mind fills with dread as time passes. What if Ruth is discovered? What if she takes care of our Masie Winters problem and is unable to do the other thing I asked her to do? The weight of the conversation we had last night hits me, but I still have no regrets.

"Are you okay?" Beth is staring at me.

"I'm fine." While I'm stuffing the empty wrapper into my backpack the fog begins to thin. "Um… Beth…"

Our fog cover has disappeared in mere seconds.

*What the hell?!*

Footsteps are marching in our direction. Lots of footsteps.

"We have to move," Beth says. "Run!"

And so we do. Through the forest, with whispers and footsteps close behind. The forest is a very different place without the fog, and at least we won't collide with any trees. Feeling confident, I glance over my shoulder and see…

*Masies!*

"At least we know we're back in our Garden!" I shout.

Except that they pulled a trick out of their hats and removed our safety fog cover.

"Come back!" one yells.

"Where are we going?" the other Syn is freaking out.

This is all new to her, like it once was for me.

"The house!" Beth grabs her hand. "Don't slow down, they're gaining on us!"

A few minutes later, we have to slow down to carefully pick our way through tangled branches. After a few more awkward climbs over, under, and around jagged branches, we enter the Square, breathless, bruised, scratched, and triumphant.

Butterfly-Man, Rat-Girl, and Snake-Man are playing a game of cards in front of the well. People were murdered yesterday. The Garden's entire population is threatened and these three are playing a casual game of *Go Fish*?

The other Syn slows her pace when she sees Snake-Man. "Oh my god. What is that?"

Beth groans. "Never mind. Keep moving."

We pass them, much to the other Syn's relief, trampling through flower beds and scraping ourselves on more bushes.

"Help!"

"Hey, let me go!"

"Syn, help!"

The other Syn has been captured by two Masies. Beth too.

"Look out, Syn!" screams Beth.

Too late. Two Masies catch me from behind.

"I'm surprised to see you here," one of them says.

More than a dozen have surrounded us and more will surely come.

BLAM!

Ruth is creeping alongside the pond with her gun. "Let them go. All of them!"

"You're with them?" one Masie asks?

"Let them go!" she repeats.

"We can't do that."

BLAM, BLAM!

The Masie holding the other Syn screams when a bullet lodges in her foot, allowing my other to escape.

Ruth points her gun at my captors. "So, it's going to be like that, huh?"

"It is."

"Get your filthy hands off of me," Beth yells.

"I will only tell you one more time. Let them go," Ruth says. "Now!"

Their grip loosens and I'm free. So is Beth. Still, Masies are circling like wolves.

"Those guns are fairly useless here," one says.

"The pain will only be temporary," says another.

Why are they talking to us as if we don't know that?

"There are two Syns now. He will be delighted."

*Who the hell is **he**?*

The circle of Masies separates, creating a path to freedom. They're letting us through. No, they are letting someone else through.

To my horror, I see who *he* is. A face from my past. The two-faced boy I never thought I would ever see again.

*Cole.*

This isn't the Garden I know. The good news is that it has healing properties. The bad news is that we have arrived in an alternate Garden where alternate versions of my worst enemies are still alive.

# Chapter 42

# DOWN THE RABBIT HOLE

"WELL, WELL, well," Cole taunts. "If it isn't Synthia Wade. Didn't think I would ever see you again, and now there are two of you." A tear spills down his cheek.

*Wait, is he crying?*

Ruth shields her Syn and me, and aims her gun at Cole.

Cole defies Ruth's gun by shifting his attention to Beth. "And who is this little badass?" He's talking about her like she's an infant.

"A little badass pointing a gun at your head."

"Adorable."

"Please let me shoot him."

"Whoa, whoa, whoa." One of the Masies holds up her hands and steps between Beth and Cole. "No one needs to shoot anyone."

Beth seems confused. "Do you really *not* know who I am?"

"We've never seen you before. But we recognize…both…Synthias."

Cole opens his mouth to speak, but is shushed by a Masie wearing a teal blouse.

"Lower your weapons so we can have a civilized conversation," Teal-Blouse Masie orders.

"We will not lower our weapons."

"Didn't we just mention that guns are rather useless here?" Teal-Blouse Masie says.

"Not if I aim for just the right spot in your skull."

Teal-Blouse Masie faces Cole. "Run to the house and bring our guests some refreshments."

"I'm not your errand boy," Cole whines.

Every Masie glares at Cole.

"Lemonade coming right up. Maybe iced-tea." A spooked Cole strolls away. "Or warm tap water," he mumbles.

"Listen," Teal-Blouse Masie says once Cole is out of earshot. "Why don't you tell us why you are here and we will do our best to accommodate you."

"We are just passing through," Ruth says. "We were trying to enter another Garden."

"Interesting. What is that Garden like?"

"It's very similar to this one," I reply, and point in Cole's direction. "But in our Garden that two-faced snake is dead."

"Ah, you have a history with Coleus. Yes, he can be cruel. The trick is to treat him like a pet. Demand his obedience."

Ruth is about to say something but I speak first, my curiosity getting the best of me. "What are you all doing in this Garden, and why is Cole alive?"

Ruth shoots me a disapproving look.

"We arrived a few days ago," Teal-Blouse Masie says. "The two-faced psychopath was running things like a dictatorship, taking his anger out on the residents because he lost a loved one in an experiment gone awry."

"The same thing happened in our Garden," I say.

"The experiment Cole lost his love to involved another version of you, whom he brought to this Garden. She didn't survive, and yet here you are. Both of you."

"Oh"

"Like I said," Ruth goes on, "we are just passing through. Is that a problem?"

"I don't see why it would be. We mean you no harm. And you are one of us, after all."

They seem sincere, but why were they chasing us? Do they have the same goal as the Masies in our Garden? If so, perhaps since they have only been here for a few days, they don't know that I am the missing link in their crazy plan to gain immortality.

Cole returns from his mission, fuming, and throws four plastic water bottles to the ground. "You promised me, and now here they are—*two* of them!"

"What is Ugly talking about?" Beth aligns her weapon with Cole's chest.

"They promised me!" Cole is screaming like a child having a temper tantrum. "They promised that if I helped them they would find me one of you, to have all to myself."

"One of us?" the other Syn asks.

"Yes," Teal-Blouse Masie says. "We promised to locate and provide him with a Synthia Wade to replace the one he lost."

*Is that why they were chasing us?*

"Either one of these will do. I'm not picky."

*Ew.*

Another Masie, this one wearing a red blouse, approaches Ruth. "Would you be willing to part with one of your Synthia's? One should be sufficient for whatever you require."

*What the hell!?!*

"That is out of the question," Ruth exclaims.

*Phew.*

"How unfortunate," Red-Blouse Masie says. "We will, however, allow you through the Garden. Cole will have to wait a little longer for his prize."

"No! You promised. There are *two*. I just want *one*!"

It's hard to decide which Cole is worse—the murderous, revenge-driven Cole or this pervy temper-tantrum iteration.

"Remember, Cole," one Masie says, "you need us a lot more than we need you."

"There are plenty of helpers in the Garden," says another.

"You may be more trouble than you are worth," Teal-Blouse Masie says.

Cole cowers on the spot. "I can be patient."

The Masies make an exit path from their circle for Cole. He scans their army, hoping for sympathy from at least one of them. Nothing. Slouching like an old man, Cole slinks away with his metaphorical tail dragging behind him.

There is a long, awkward moment of many minds wondering what to do next. The other Syn watches Cole's departing figure, shaking her head.

"Alright then," Red-Blouse Masie says. "You must want to be on your way."

"Unless you'd be interested in staying here and joining us," Teal-Blouse Masie says.

*Oh hell no.*

"I assure you, it would be well worth your time," she adds.

"Thank you for the offer," Ruth says, "but we'll be leaving now."

"As you wish."

The Masies break into small groups, strolling in the same direction as Cole. His figure is now a tiny silhouette.

"Well, that was creepy," the other Syn says. "Dozens of Masie lookalikes and their pervy two-faced bitch."

It's fascinating how different this Syn is from me. She uses vulgar language a lot more, though I must admit in this case it's quite apropos.

"This was nothing compared to the dangers I fear are coming," Ruth says. "That is why I wanted you to stay at home."

The other Syn shrugs. "Well, I'm here now. Let's go find that Garden."

"What do we do now?" Beth asks.

I catch Ruth's eyes. "Look for the rabbit hole?"

"That's right."

"What should we be looking for, exactly?" Beth asks.

"We will know it when we see it," is all Ruth will say.

We spread out and search the Garden for the rabbit hole. We get a lot of odd looks because we are not strangers to the residents, and yet we are—two girls identical to a girl who died here, and one Masie who isn't part of the pack.

*I can't wait to get out of here.*

A few minutes pass and then the other Syn says, "Over there! Is that it?"

Something is glimmering across the pond, near a cabin.

"That's it!"

As we approach, a bright circular light is glowing where grass should be. Unlike the lightway I'm used to, it doesn't beam upwards.

Ruth raises her arms to stop us from getting too close. "This rabbit hole will take us from one Garden to another. Not necessarily the Garden we intend to reach, so we have to be cautious."

"It's right out in the open," I observe. "Far from the fog."

"Unfortunately." Ruth says. "Just be careful, and be quiet. We'll head to the fog no matter what Garden we end up in. Understood?"

We all nod.

"Alright. Once I have gone through, each of you take your turn."

The instant Ruth moves into the glowing circle of light, she sinks as if falling into an actual rabbit hole.

"So, um," the other Syn mumbles. "Who wants to go next?"

Without a word, Beth leaps into the light as if she's diving into a pool.

"You go next," I tell the other Syn.

Her eyes widen.

"Or, I can go and leave you here alone."

She scrunches her eyes shut and sidesteps into the glowing circle.

I hope that we land in our Garden, or at least in one where healing properties exist. I inhale the heavenly oxygen and inch forward into the light. Just as my eyes drop below the surface, I am lifted up like in an elevator and reunited with my clan.

We huddle with our backs to each other, attempting to make out our surroundings. This is incredibly difficult because we are immersed in thick fog, but not the fog on the outskirts of the Garden we're used to. I am certain we have landed smack dab in the middle of the Garden.

There are voices in the distance. The other Syn gasps as our ears are pierced by the sound of someone screaming. Beth staggers into us when the ground starts to shake, accompanied by an eerily familiar rumbling sound. My other shrieks and squeezes my hand.

"You have *got* to be kidding me," says Beth, as the other Syn's eyes widen again. "Still glad you followed us?"

"What is that sound?" the other Syn screeches, running to the comfort of Ruth's arms.

"The roar of a beast."

*A monster.*

# Chapter 43

# A MONSTER CALLS

HOW DID THE MONSTER GET here from the valley? Does this fog cover the entire Garden? Lightways are flashing in the distance just like in the Garden I know, but one thing is for certain—this is not *my* Garden. I can breathe easily so at least there are healing properties here.

"Is somebody going to tell me what that was?" the other Syn demands, flinching as the monster roars again.

Ruth takes her hand. "Just. Don't. Look. At. It. Do you understand?"

*Where have I heard that before?*

The other Syn gulps. "Okay."

"Stay close, everyone. Be ready for anything."

Beth and Ruth have their guns ready. I choose to keep mine tucked away. I hate those things, and don't trust my skills to shoot through this thick fog.

"Okay, time to find another rabbit hole," says Ruth.

I bet each one of us wants to run with every monstrous roar, but we have to be careful when traveling with such poor visibility. If I have my bearings right, we are headed for the empty field next to the house. The orchard should be just ahead. Ruth must be guessing that the trees will give us some cover.

The other Syn is startled by each flash of a lightway, and she looks back whenever the monster roars. She's making me more nervous than I normally would be. The monster sounds close, but I think…or hope…that it's at the other end of the Garden, which would place it near the bog.

There hasn't been any more screaming, but occasionally I hear whispering. We pass by the lightways because we are Garden hopping not world hopping. With the rabbit hole being on the ground, it will be especially difficult to locate in this fog.

I'm startled when someone brushes past me. There is something familiar about the figure's form. "Luke?"

He studies my face and the rest of us, and moves on.

"Was that Luke?"

"Yes," Beth says, "and no."

I understand. This Luke is likely one of the humans my alternate parents who created this Garden brought over. He only looked at me because I called out. He didn't recognize us or the name. I wonder if versions of Ebby and Jon could have been plucked from their worlds and brought here, or to some other Garden?

I thought I had seen it all, but apparently not. Now I am traveling through alternate Gardens with another version of Aunt Ruth and myself, and trying not to get eaten by a monster.

It seems that we will have to try extra hard to protect ourselves because when we reach the orchard, any hope of shelter is lost. All the fruit trees are nothing more than stumps. I wonder if anything has been left standing in this Garden.

BOOM, BOOM, BOOM!

The monster is close. My legs go weak at the sound of more screaming. Two humans, or Creepers, rush past too quickly for me to see their faces in the fog.

"Do we have a plan?" I shout.

"Run!"

We sprint through the field that leads to the house, narrowly avoiding a lightway. Traveling to an alternate world from this strange Garden would be a major hiccup in the plan to return to ours.

BOOM, BOOM, BOOM!

*Though it may be the only way to avoid being eaten by this monster!*

Beth and I keep stumbling into each other every time the ground shakes.

"We're almost at the house," she yells above another monstrous roar.

Except that the house isn't even standing. It's nothing more than a pile of rubble. The house has been demolished and the wood left to rot. I'm unsure how the healing properties remain, but am very glad that they do.

BOOM, BOOM, BOOM!

Damn, it's close. Ruth leads us past the wreckage and we huddle within the rubble.

BOOM, BOOM, BOOM! CRUNCH, CRUNCH!

The monster is stomping through the rubble.

*It's right behind us!*

"Don't look at it!" Ruth shouts. "Just run!"

We trample through the flattened brush to the pond. Another lightway appears. Can we reach it in time?

BOOM, BOOM, BOOM!

"Run to the lightway!" Ruth shouts.

"But…" Beth trails off, confused.

"We have no choice!"

Ruth is right. This lightway will take us to another world, not another Garden. And it may be the only way we can get out of here alive. We are maybe sixty feet away by the time the lightway finishes its second flashing sequence.

BOOM, BOOM, BOOM!

"Hurry!"

The lightway finishes its third sequence. The fourth and final sequence begins, the beam of light holding still. The ground rumbles and I trip, running headlong into the other Syn.

"We can still make it!" Beth screams. She helps us up and we keep running.

*Four seconds from the lightway!*

BOOM, BOOM, BOOM!

SPLASH!

"Beth!" I stop in my tracks, facing the very realization that I am about to be that beastly Creeper's food. My sister has fallen into the pond. I can't leave her.

BOOM, BOOM, BOOM!

The ominous silhouette of the monster is charging through the fog and it's so close I can hardly keep my balance. I have felt like I was about to die on several occasions, but there are no words to describe the terror of knowing your body is about to be mangled by gigantic razor-sharp teeth.

# Chapter 44

# GONE

JUST AS HEAT FROM THE monster's breath hits my face, someone pushes me into the pond. Two more splashes follow. Ruth and the other Syn!

The monster's roar is so loud my ears are ringing. I grab hold of a tree root that's protruding from the side of the pond, managing to keep myself afloat and hidden as deeply underwater as possible.

The monster is sniffing dangerously close, its hideous breath wafting up my nostrils. I hold my breath and hope that I don't vomit. My hands are starting to cramp and I can't hold on much longer. Luckily, our scents must be masked by the murky water because the monster seems to have given up.

It swings around to leave and I duck when its humongous tail nearly lops off my head before it splashes into the water. The monster turns back, thinking its prey is on the move. My hands are cramping like crazy! I can't hold on anymore. My heart leaps as my grip is lost and I start splashing in panic.

The monster roars again, thankfully masking my splashing noises. I peek above the surface and sure enough, it's slinking away.

When it's out of earshot, I whisper, "It's gone!"

Beth pops up next to me and Ruth helps the other Syn swim over.

"Now what?" the other Syn asks.

"We climb out of here and keep looking for the rabbit hole," Ruth says.

"I don't think so," Beth says, smirking.

"What? Why not?" the other Syn gripes.

My sister is pointing to where the lightway we were running to was.

"Beth, the lightway is gone," says Ruth.

"I know. Look again."

Just behind where the lightway was is a circle of light embedded in the grass, resembling a glowing Frisbee.

"Excellent!" Ruth claps her hands.

The monster roars. We stand there laughing, because we know we have time to.

BOOM, BOOM, BOOM!

*All right, time to go.*

"I'd love to stay for dinner," shouts Beth, "but I'm not fond of what's on the menu." She drops into the rabbit role.

I wait for Ruth and the other Syn to take their turns. Then, facing the fog, I inch backwards to the glowing ball of light. When the monster's silhouette reappears, charging through the fog, I stagger into the light. Just like before, once my head is beneath the surface I rise into a new Garden.

My allies and I are standing next to the pond. There is no fog. The sky is red, there are sparks in the air, and a sliver of light is flashing in the distance.

Beth is glancing in every direction, even up and down.

My chest is still free of congestion. This sure seems like the Garden we left.

The other Syn is hunched over, vomiting, having turned her back on a mangled corpse. I watch Ruth comfort her, totally disgusted and unable to stop my last memories of Lily and Mom from resurfacing.

Another wasted life, thrown to their death from Doom World.

Ruth points to the southern part of the Garden, opposite where the house is situated, and we're off again.

Although I can't see a soul, voices around us are unmistakable. Our little group is not alone. We stay close together while walking to the Square, carefully observing our surroundings and staying as far away as possible from the voices.

"Oh my god!" the other Syn yelps, turning away.

Beth and Ruth shush her.

Another poor soul is falling from the sky. Ruth narrows her brow as if suddenly realizing something, and we share a fleeting glance.

This isn't a surprise to her. We spoke about how people are thrown to their deaths from Doom World; how they are tossed into the massive hole created when land was ripped out by our parents to form the Garden, and then fall through the lightway on the other side of the Oblivion.

*I wonder what has Ruth so deep in thought.*

We reach the end of the Square without seeing any humans or Creepers, and most importantly, no Masies. As we pass the well, I notice something different from the Garden I'm hoping we've reached.

There is no fog blanketing the forest. Either we are in another alternate Garden, or this is the Garden we intended to return to and the Masies have somehow removed the fog.

Ruth leads us into the forest. We are no longer protected by the elements of the fog, which prevented us from being easily seen or heard from outside the forest. I didn't realize how strange the forest was without the chirping of birds and the scurrying of small animals. All of these little critters stayed out of the fog. This forest is rather pleasant now.

Ruth gathers us into a huddle. "Is this the Garden you left?"

I'm about to tell her that I don't know, but Beth replies first.

"It is."

"How do you know?"

Beth points to three tree stumps. "The same trees were cut down in our Garden."

It blows my mind how she remembers which trees have been cut down, especially since we could barely see our hands in front of us when the fog covered the forest.

"The trees could have been cut down in an alternate Garden too," Ruth says. "We need to know for certain."

"How can we find out?" I ask.

"I can blend in," Ruth says. "What should I look for?"

"Nothing."

A voice from above startles us, and Ruth and Beth raise their guns.

"Don't shoot!" I whisper, more loudly than intended.

"Thanks, Syn." Maya's only surviving child lowers himself on a strand of web.

The other Syn recoils.

"This is Jeremy. He's a friend."

Jeremy has grown since my last visit to the Garden. When we first met, he was the size of a normal spider. Now he is an appropriate size for a human his age, rather formidable to a newcomer like the other Syn. The last time I saw him, he and his mother were piercing their fangs into Cole, taking revenge for the murder of Jeremy's siblings and father.

Jeremy is puzzled. "There are two of you. And you're with one of *them*!

"I'm not one of them," says Ruth. "I'm here to help."

"I heard you've been jumping between Gardens. You want to know that you have returned to the correct Garden, right?"

"How do you know this?"

"Well for starters, I overheard your conversation. But also, my mom knew that's what you would be up to. She says you are predictable."

I roll my eyes.

"Speaking of Mom, I better go before she realizes I'm talking to you." He turns away, pauses, and turns back with sad eyes. "I'm sorry about your mom and Lily. I liked them both."

My eyes are brimming with tears as Jeremy zips up on his web. I had hoped that maybe through some miracle, Mom had survived after we left.

Beth wipes away a few tears too. "She is really gone."

Ruth waits while we hold each other for a few minutes, and then touches us on the shoulders. "I'm sorry girls. It seems that Jeremy has confirmed that with all probability, this is the Garden we targeted. That means you all must stay hidden. The trees are thick here, so stay put and wait until I return. I'll do what has to be done."

"Will you be okay when the sound frequency is turned on?"

"I'm not turning on the sound frequency. I have a new plan."

"What?"

"Finding the exact frequency to affect my others' nervous systems will be time-consuming. I can only blend in for so long before they realize something is up."

"So what are you going to do?"

"Just know that when I am done there won't be time for goodbyes. I will come for my Syn and we will escape as quickly as possible."

I want to know more, but it's probably better I don't.

"Beth, you and your sister are brave young women." Ruth gives her Syn a big hug. "Promise me you will stay hidden."

"I promise."

"If the whole thing goes sideways and I don't return, stay with our new friends. Travel to their world if you can or return to ours through a sliver of light."

The other Syn's lower lip trembles as Ruth leaves.

I have an urge to do something. "Beth, I'll be right back."

Beth peeks out from behind the tree where she's hiding. "Where are you going?"

"Trust me. Just stay here."

As quietly as possible, I catch up with Ruth, safely out of Beth's earshot.

"Syn, what are you doing?"

"That thing we talked about. You'll do it, right?"

Ruth looks concerned and a strong feeling of déjà vu washes over me. This exact moment appeared as one of the projections I saw while falling through the Oblivion!

*Aunt Ruth…In the Garden?! I lean close to tell her something. She looks terribly concerned.*

I give my head a shake.

"Are you certain, Synthia? If I do this, there is no going back."

I might change my mind after returning to my world, and regret asking her to do this. Of course there are strong doubts and for that reason I spit out two words before those doubts change my mind: "I'm certain."

"I will do everything in my power to fulfil your request."

As I'm tiptoeing back to my hiding spot I am second-guessing myself already. There is surely a reason why the Oblivion projected that moment before it occurred. When I spotted the Masies through my window, that led to Aunt Ruth's death and everything we have been through since my visions. I may have just made the biggest mistake of my life.

"What was that about?" Beth whispers.

"I'll tell you later," I lie.

Although I feel Beth's narrowed eyes targeting me, I focus on the other Syn. She's scared, yet excited. If all goes as hoped, we will soon say goodbye. It may seem egotistical to like a virtual clone of yourself. While we share many experiences, and of course our DNA, she is her own person. I have grown fond of her.

Could this really be the end of our troubles? If Ruth can blend in with the Masies and complete her task, Beth and I can finally return home.

Suddenly, there is a tapping sound on a nearby tree. Beth leaps into action, aiming her gun in multiple directions.

"Relax, Beth. It's just Flint."

"Syn!" He flings himself at me and lifts me into a bear hug. "I'm so glad you're safe!"

"We have to be really quiet," I whisper.

He puts me down, grinning. "Okay."

If Flint can find us, anyone can. This may not go as smoothly as I'd hoped.

Flint sits down, his smile fading. "Syn, we have to talk." He pats the ground beside him and I sit.

Beth stands guard, leaning against a nearby tree. The other Syn is sitting against another tree, lost in thought, most likely concerned about Ruth.

"What do you want to talk about?"

"After you and Beth left, the Masies promised they wouldn't kill anyone else if we captured you and turned you in. Some humans and Creepers agreed. They believe it's their only hope for survival."

*I'm not surprised.*

"I hate to ask this…" he falters, "have you thought about turning yourself in?"

"If they get their hands on me, the Garden will be destroyed. Everyone here will die."

"I figured there had to be a reason why you took off. You wouldn't have left us behind with them otherwise."

"Don't worry, Flint. This should all be over quickly."

While he's hugging me again, my ears pick up the faint sound of something being dragged across the ground.

Beth is frantic. "Syn is gone!"

"No!"

Flint is confused, but doesn't have time to ask questions.

I leave Flint behind and race through the forest with Beth. I'm pretty certain we're following the trail they've made and sure enough, there she is. The other Syn is being dragged away by something attached to her ankles—strands of spider silk.

# Chapter 45

# WEB OF BETRAYAL

MY FIRST THOUGHT IS THAT Jeremy betrayed us, but then I realize it wasn't him.

It was Maya.

The other Syn is terrified, but she can't scream because her mouth is webbed shut. She should be scared. I know where Maya is taking her.

Beth and I continue the chase at top speed, almost plowing into someone who has dropped down from above.

"Jeremy!"

He glances in the direction that Maya is dragging the other Syn, but they are both out of sight. Jeremy's surprise is evident. He had no clue about his mother's betrayal.

"Out of our way!" Beth shouts.

"Wait! That's the other Syn my mom took, right? This is good. She didn't see that there are two of you."

"No, Jeremy. I won't let her die. Her life matters just as much as mine."

"I don't care about *her*. I care about *you*."

Beth aims her gun at Jeremy, angry enough to use it.

"Listen, Jeremy. That girl shares my exact DNA. It doesn't matter which one of us the Masies get. The result will be the same."

"Yeah," Jeremy says. "We will all be safe."

"No, you moron," Beth says. "If they get either Syn, everyone in the Garden dies!"

"Huh?" He looks at me for confirmation.

"She's right."

Jeremy's eyes widen and his lower lip begins to tremble. "They put that other you in the chair…"

"The other me? You mean Synister?"

"Yeah. It was horrible!"

"Is she…alive?

"No. There was barely anything left of her when they were done. But we didn't die."

"That's because she's too sick for the procedure to work. They used her as a lab rat for a trial run."

Beth pushes past him, disgusted.

We don't have time to take the long route through the forest, let alone stand around and mourn Synister. We must cross through the Garden and hope no one stops us. Surely, every Masie will already be at that chair contraption.

I pull out my handgun and hope its presence is enough to deter anyone from getting in our way. But we can't let anyone stop us, or we all die.

Trees are a blur while we sprint through the forest. We pick up speed through the Square because there are fewer trees to navigate around. As we trot alongside the pond, I notice several humans and Creepers have gathered by one of the cabins. They're shocked to see us. Too shocked to get in our way, but we make sure our guns are easily noticeable just in case.

The back of the house is visible above the trees ahead. Before we exit the path to the house, I stop Beth.

"We need a plan before we rush in. Otherwise, they will—"

BOOM!

In unison with the thunderous boom, menacing clouds swiftly blanket the red sky. Except for the faint red glow behind the clouds, it's almost as dark as night. There are continuous strikes of lightning, each one illuminating the sparks in the air. The clouds burst torrents down on us. Hailstones plummet our faces.

The Masies' procedure has begun. There's no time to wait for Ruth's plan to be carried out. If we don't do something right away, not only will the other Syn die, but the Masies will be transported to the Tether World. After that, the Garden and everyone in it will be no more.

Cowering from the painful onslaught of ice pellets, we dash past the stairway and through the carport, stopping short as a horde of Masies has congregated in front of the house. Hundreds are gathered within the sparkling light show.

"There's no way we'll ever get past all of them," Beth shouts over the hailstorm.

"What are you going to do?" A new voice startles me.

I almost draw my gun…on Jeremy. "You trying to get yourself killed?"

"No, you guys are trying to get yourselves killed," he says. "I have a suggestion."

"You going to web them all up?" Beth challenges sarcastically.

"No, even better." His eyes are twinkling as they reflect the sparks in the air.

Beth puts her hands on her hips.

Jeremy motions to the roof of the house. Next thing we know, two Creeper birds have landed in front of us.

"Get on!" Jeremy shouts, above the hammers of the hailstorm.

The Creeper birds are not enthused.

"I don't know about this."

"You have a better idea?" Jeremy says, eyeing several Masies who are approaching.

"Point taken." On tiptoe, I take hold of a couple of scales and climb up the Creeper like I'm ascending a ladder, then loop my arms around its neck. It's going to be a struggle to stay on this wet, scaly beast.

Jeremy is helping Beth climb onto her ride while a vast number of Garden residents look on. They have congregated with some of the Masies for the show, wrongly assuming that sacrificing me will save them.

Jeremy's ear-piercing whistle jolts the Creeper birds into action. They raise their heads and rise off the ground.

From up here, the lightning bolts are as red as the sky was. I strain to see through the dim light. A crowd has gathered below, mulling around that souped up chair in the open green space next to the house. The other Syn is sitting in the chair with her head inside the metal helmet. Electrical currents are zapping her body.

*We're too late!*

The Creeper birds circle above the crowd and lower their heads. I'm wet and freezing, and the landing is rough, but I hang on until we have come to a full stop. By the time I've slid off, a pack of Masies is closing in. They're confused, glancing back and forth between me and the immobilized Syn.

BLAM!

Beth shoots a bullet into the air. The Creeper birds create a barrier between us and the crowd. Their crocodile-like mouths are gaping with large dagger teeth ready to chomp on anyone who gets too close.

The residents are uncertain of their next move and the Masies have no direction to give them. Their advance has come to a standstill. The now red electrical currents are still zapping the other Syn's body.

BLAM!

Beth shoots again, this time at the ground. She's shooting bullets through the thick wire protruding from the chair.

One Masie manages to sneak between the Creeper birds during the shooting commotion and attacks Beth from behind, kicking her gun from her hand. It flies towards a couple of Masies. They reach for it, but have second thoughts as Beth charges at them.

Now I have no choice but to pull out my gun to hold off the Masies. I truly don't want to shoot anyone, and am startled when a shot rings out. A Masie screams and crouches in the grass, clutching her leg.

*I didn't pull the trigger…did I?*

Beth is holding a smoking gun and has already raced to the chair. She fires another bullet into the cord and sparks fly. The impact knocks her off her feet which causes her to lose her grip on the gun.

"I'm fine!" she shouts. "Finish what I started!"

The Creeper birds are distracted. One is mauling a Masie. The other is flying away with his "meal". Beth is on the ground, disarmed. The other Syn's fate is up to me now. Can she still be saved? Hail is pelting against her helmet. Electrical currents are zapping her every thirty seconds or so.

*If only she hadn't followed us to the Garden.*

There's a panel directly behind her head, with wires jutting from it. I take aim and fire, and almost shoot Beth when a Masie knocks me off balance.

BLAM!

I got her!

The Masie yelps and grabs her bloody shoulder.

I aim my gun at the metal casing. Beth finds her dropped gun and joins me. I nod and we both shoot, again and again. Sparks fly from the chair and sizzle out, as do the electrical currents around the other Syn.

The hail has ceased and the sky is a typical daytime blue. The slivers of light and sparks in the air are gone. Not gone, are the throngs of Masies. And, we're out of bullets.

"You haven't stopped us!"

"We will rebuild and repeat the procedure!"

Their voices are muffled by my concern for the other Syn. Her eyes are shut and she is completely still. She has stopped breathing.

Ruth frantically pushes through the mob of like-faced women and kneels by her side, wrought with emotion, and trying not to show in front of the Masies. She pretends to examine the figure in the chair, while her heart is obviously breaking.

Overcome with sadness for Ruth, and disbelief, I can only gape at the other Syn in that horrible chair. I feel Beth's hand on my shoulder and my grief is softened.

I can't afford to be distracted by grief anyway. The Masies and Garden residents are closing in around us.

# Chapter 46

# ALL THE LIGHT
# WE CANNOT SEE

WE'RE TRAPPED AGAINST THE CHAIR that holds the other Syn's lifeless body. There's no way to escape. The hundreds of Masies surrounding us are enraged and more than ready to take that rage out on Beth and me.

Out of nowhere, Maya's eight legs hit the ground in front of us. "You had your chance to stay away, Synthia Wade. Your unfortunate demise is no one's fault but your own."

"No Mom!" Jeremy is climbing along a strand of web that's stretched from the roof of the house to a tree. "They lied to us. If their plan is successful, we die too!"

"It's true," I say. "The Masies plan to absorb the healing properties of my DNA with that chair. If they succeed, the Garden will disappear. Me, you, Jeremy—everyone will cease to exist."

"Liar!" A chorus of residents waves angry arms.

"Don't listen to her!" shouts another resident.

Ruth faces the crowd, standing tall with renewed strength. "This girl speaks the truth! They…we…will live forever. This is what we have been working for. We will have immunity to all illnesses in the Tether World and this Garden and everyone in it will cease to exist."

Make-Up Masie's smile disappears as she realizes that Ruth isn't one of them. There are gasps and murmurs from the Garden residents. Some back away from the Masies, wide-eyed. Some run. Others are rooted in place, regarding the Masies with pure hatred. Punches are thrown, but Masies vastly outnumber Garden residents.

Amidst the commotion, Beth, Ruth, and I are huddled beside the other Syn's chair. The Creeper birds have flown away. Then, I hear a most familiar cough and quickly turn to face the chair.

"Ruth, Beth, she's alive!"

*Saved by the Garden's healing properties!*

Ruth lays her head upon her Syn's chest. "Oh, thank god. You're my everything." She glances at me. "We don't have much time."

As we begin to unbuckle the straps, Beth is yanked backwards by a Masie.

"Get your hands off of me!" Beth yells.

The Masie is trying to strangle Beth. "You won't stop us!"

My sister's arms are flailing, trying to grab Masie's throat. She's starting to choke!

"Let her go!"

There's a battle cry, and from the mass of rioting residents and Masies, Mitchell charges to Beth's aid, whacking her captor in the back of her head with a long metal shovel. Beth is freed, but can only sit there rubbing her throat.

I drop the last belt from the other Syn's leg and it dangles from the chair. Beth is coughing and coughing, sounding just like me. I glance at her with concern, but she waves me off impatiently.

I remove the other Syn's helmet and Ruth lifts her into her arms.

"We don't have a second to waste. Pull the metal disc from my bag!"

I unzip the backpack and pull out the metal object, and then lay it on the ground in front of Ruth.

"Synthia!" Ruth must yell to be heard above the chaos. "I am not the woman who raised you. But I surely speak for her when I say how sorry she was. Know that she always loved you. I will always love you too."

I can find no words.

She smiles at the gratitude in my eyes and steps onto the disc. A bright lightway bolts upwards.

"Watch the sky. When it happens, get to cover." She goes into the light with the other Syn, her smile fading with the lightway.

I stop waving goodbye. "Ruth, did you…?"

Though Ruth and the other Syn are fading quickly, I swear that the bottom of Ruth's chin lowers ever so slightly in a nod. Seconds later, Ruth and her Syn are gone.

At least a dozen Masies have encircled us now, and there is not one thing we can do about it.

"We need you," says one.

My arms are thrust behind my back.

"But we don't need your sister."

I'm pulled away from Beth, who is being restrained in a headlock.

"It didn't have to come to this, Synthia."

*She's going to break Beth's neck! An instant, permanent death!*

I try to escape with every ounce of strength that's left, kicking and biting and twisting. My shoulders ache from the strain.

"Syn," Beth pleads, as they force her to bend over.

*This isn't goodbye. It can't be!*

"Let her go!" I scream, louder than ever in my whole life. Every ounce of my being is filled with some strange power, so strong that I wrench myself free and shove my captors to the ground.

Then something strange happens. The Masies holding Beth and those trapped in Maya's webs, plus the hordes fighting Garden residents, stop moving. Every one of them is immobilized. The Masies' motionless forms begin to glow, as if they are lightways.

Beth pries herself free. "What's happening?"

"Ruth's plan! She was successful."

Every Masie glows brighter until the light is blinding. I have to shield my eyes. The light emitting from them flickers out. Hundreds of glowing Masies have vanished.

The residents, bruised, battered, and highly confused, carefully help each other up off the ground, frowning with disbelief.

Ruth's final words echo through my mind.

*When it happens, get to cover.*

I know what Ruth has done, and what we have to do.

"Get to cover," I mumble, trying to assert myself. Numb with shock, I gaze at Beth. "When it happens…"

"What?"

Beth can't hear me because I'm unable to speak loudly enough. Ruth's face flashes into memory, speaking her last words again.

"Get to cover!" I say, louder this time.

The residents nearby are wide-eyed.

I find my voice. "Everyone, get to cover!"

# Chapter 47

# THE WICKED SHALL FALL

"ONE MINUTE. TWO…tops."

Beth shakes me. "What are you talking about?"

Things have gotten crazy again—as if they had ever been normal. People are talking over each other, trying to figure out what just happened and if it's over.

No, it isn't quite over. The Masies are coming back, and their return will hit hard. Literally.

"Beth, there's no time to explain. Trust me. We have to find cover!"

We run around yelling for people to take cover. Maybe twenty out of the dozens of Garden residents are heeding our warning.

I point to the sky. "There they are!"

Beth squints to see what I'm pointing at.

Not much more than pin dots, but they are coming. Hundreds of Masies who vanished are about to rain down upon us. Ruth sent them into the lightway we traveled through after jumping off the bridge in Doom World and falling through the Oblivion. Amazingly we survived with a makeshift parachute. They are not so lucky.

Beth screams and points to the small dots that are growing exponentially as they approach. "We need to move…now!"

There's more confusion than action.

Beth nudges me. "We have to go."

Butterfly-Man rises above the crowd, pointing to the sky. The crowd hushes somewhat as some residents take notice. Still, nobody has moved.

Hogan pushes to the middle of the crowd. He points to the sky and in his booming voice shouts, "If you don't move from this area, you will die."

Now everyone is in panic mode. The Masies are clearly in sight above us, arms and legs flailing, plummeting closer.

"Don't panic! Just run!" Butterfly-Man shouts, flapping his wings above us.

"Follow those girls!" yells Crystal.

Beth and I lead the pack to the orchard. Maya springs out of sight on a silken thread, Jeremy clinging to her back. Residents and Creepers run into the forest, some take cover in nearby buildings.

The Masies' screams are growing louder with each passing second. It's a sound that sends shivers up and down my spine and threatens to stop me in my tracks. I have to cover my ears. My legs feel like lead.

*Are we going fast enough? Will we make it?*

I stupidly uncover my ears. The ensuing sounds will be with me to the end of time. Yelping and wailing. Bodies thumping to the ground, smashing through trees and crashing through rooftops, and the crackling of shattering spines.

I keep running even after it registers that the horrific wailing and bone smashing sounds have stopped.

"Syn!"

I spin around.

Beth has stopped running and is trying to catch her breath. "It's…over."

I look across the Garden, which has become a graveyard of Masie Winters. Bodies are bent out of shape, strewn around the grounds like a battlefield.

It's just too much.

I'm overcome with gratitude at the sight of Lundy running across the grass. The Masies didn't kill him while we were gone! The sight of him brings great comfort and I let him wrap me in his arms.

Flint and Rose are sitting on the ground nearby. Flint has buried his face in his mother's arms and is being rocked back and forth like a baby.

"Is it over?" asks Rose quietly.

"It appears so." Maya and Jeremy swing down on a strand of web.

"We better check the bodies," Beth says, "to make sure they're all dead."

"Your sister's right," says Larry.

Hogan groans. "Unfortunately, I agree."

"Jeremy," Maya says, "is this not the most spectacular spread? I can hardly wait to take my first sip."

I flash Maya a dirty look, which is reciprocated with a devious grin. I wave her off and trudge over to our small team of investigators.

All the bodies are twisted, backs and necks broken. Permanent deaths in this world, where death supposedly is no more. Seeing all these mangled bodies of women who look identical to the woman who raised me should make me ill. But sadly, I am getting used to death and malice. What is most disturbing is that death doesn't horrify me the way it once did. That doesn't change the fact that they killed my mother and my friend. I'm just relieved this is finally over.

Beth and I race to the house, leaping over dead bodies. Beth practically falls up the front steps in her haste, and jumps over three bodies on the main level. I nearly slip through a hole in the hardwood floor where a body crashed through the planks. I'm teetering on the edge of the hole, trying to catch my balance, when Beth yanks me to safety in the nick of time.

Some computer monitors have been smashed, but luckily the glowing blue machine that controls the Garden's healing properties has not been damaged.

Larry and Hogan are surveying around the back of the house.

Hogan looks up as we approach. "All dead."

Maya and Jeremy startle me when they drop down in front of us.

"The roof is clear," Jeremy announces.

"So much for the fail-safe," Maya says. "We could have killed them all weeks ago."

Ruth was right. They were bluffing.

"We should check the rest of the Garden," Beth says.

Lundy is jogging down the path to the pond when we round the corner of the house. My gut tells me that we should follow. Our pace quickens at the sound of kicking and splashing. Lundy is standing on the bank, clutching his gun by his side.

"No way!" Beth charges ahead.

I can't believe my eyes.

*Make-Up Masie survived!*

She is grasping at the pond bank, trying to stay afloat, her face streaked with mascara. Lundy shoves his gun against her forehead.

"Lundy, don't! We won. It's over."

Lundy's furious eyes don't falter from his target. His hand is shaking. "No, Syn. We didn't win. They killed your mom. They killed my Lily. I never knew true love until I met her."

"I loved Lily too. But she wouldn't want you to go down this path."

"Listen to her." Masie is breathless. "If her words don't convince you, let this sink in. You should be lucky I am alive. If all of us are killed there will be devastating consequences, remember?"

Lundy mocks laughter. "Because of your contingency plan?"

"I am not bluffing."

"Well, you know what?" Lundy pushes the gun harder against her forehead.

"Lundy, no!"

"I don't care."

BLAM!

The sound of the gunshot pierces through every inch of me. Masie sinks below the surface, a rippling puddle of red spreading in her wake. A bullet to the brain, or the brain being decimated in this case, means permanent death. She is not coming back.

Cloaked in defeat, Lundy drops the gun to the grass and slumps to the ground. "Lily was everything to me."

"I'm so sorry, Lundy." I sit down beside him and he leans into me, interlocking his fingers with mine and sharing my grief.

Our friends give us a private moment of silence. We both cry. Me for the loss of my mother and my good friend, and Lundy for the loss of his first love. Little by little, the splotch of blood is diluted by the pond water. My heart lurches when Lundy picks up his gun, but he whips it into the pond and it sinks.

"So, Masie *was* bluffing," Jeremy says awkwardly.

As if on cue, a loud crackling noise erupts in the center of the Garden. That noise. So familiar. Like an electrical current.

*No, no, no!*

Everybody faces the Garden in a common state of dread—dread that is soon to be justified. A voltway appears in the distance, near the spiral stairway. A pitch-black tunnel spirals to the sky, yellow and blue electrical currents encircling it. This is not just any voltway. It is wide enough to allow three full-grown elephants to enter. It's like a gateway for a giant.

A giant or…a monster.

# Chapter 48

# GATEWAY TO HELL

"IT WASN'T A BLUFF!" Lundy is panicking. "What have I done?"

"It doesn't matter," I say. "You might be—"

"It doesn't matter? You know what's coming through that thing?"

"You might be the only one who can stop it."

"How can I stop it?"

"The voltway is opened from the computer in the sewers. That is where the Masies must have gone to set up their contingency plan. You know that whole computer system better than anyone."

"They cut off my access."

"Maybe that's changed now. If not, there is no one in the house stopping you from regaining access."

"I'm sure they used passwords. How? How can I—"

I hit his shoulder with force. He's panicking and we don't have time to waste. "You did this. You said so yourself. Now that my mom is gone…" I falter, "you are the only person who can shut this down."

He doesn't respond.

"You can't go back and change what you just did. But you can take responsibility by trying to fix this. Okay?"

Lundy is trying to process.

"Can you do that?"

"I'll try." He nods, as if to reassure himself. Then, he runs.

Beth and I make a beeline for the voltway, navigating across a field of twisted and mangled bodies.

"He won't be able to close it," Beth says. "The Masies would have made sure of that."

"That doesn't mean he shouldn't try."

The crackling from the electrical currents rings through my ears as we approach the voltway. A crowd has gathered. Everyone is panicking. I suspect that most of them remember the three Garden residents who went through the voltway from the sewers and were never seen again. Except for that one arm that was returned before Lundy shut it down.

The crowd is angry when they see me.

"This is your fault!"

"You brought all this here!"

"Your friends are safe and now more of us are going to die?" Clover screams, pointing an angry finger at me. "You know what's coming, don't you?"

"Yes," I say softly. "Anyone who wants to fight this monster should gather weapons. Those not fighting should hide in the sewers with the children."

Fawn approaches. This is the first time I have seen Lily's mom since Lily was killed. "So, you're going underground to hide?" she sneers.

"No. Only to gather weapons. I'm going to fight that thing when it arrives."

Fawn gazes at me, empty of expression. Then she collapses, sobbing.

"I am so sorry."

* * *

After collecting the weapons Luke brought to the Garden for our battle against Cole, Beth and I check on Lundy.

"I can't do it. They've locked everything." Lundy throws up his hands with exasperation. "I'm going to the house. Maybe I can get access from there. But I'm certain Masie password-protected everything."

"Lundy, if you can close the voltway, a lot of lives will be saved."

He shakes his head. "Don't get your hopes up, Syn. I'm just a low-level IT guy, not a hacker."

"Don't underestimate yourself. I believe in you."

Most Garden residents have decided to stay underground. Our little army will be made up of a handful of humans and a couple dozen Creepers.

"We should stay down here too," Beth says, as we arrive at the grate that exits to the Garden. "Now that the Masies are gone, we can go home."

"I'm not running, Beth. I can't leave everyone with this monster. How could I live with myself?"

"You realize the only way to stop this monster is to kill it."

"I know."

"And you're okay with that?"

We hold each other's gaze for a long moment. Killing another living being is a horrible thought. But this monster will kill everyone or force them to live underground in the sewers again. I feel responsible and have no choice. Still, I can't admit to Beth that I am okay with killing something, because I am not. So, I say nothing.

* * *

Our small unit of fighters has strategically surrounded the giant voltway, ready for the monster's entrance. Some wonder if the creature will even come, but the Masies would not have set up a contingency plan if they weren't positive it would be successful. Considering their fail-safe would only proceed upon their demise, why would they bother unless they were certain the monster would surface and wreak havoc?

Rose, Flint, Larry, and Nell are watching safely from the platform in the sky, and will tend to the wounded if required. The hope is that the healing properties will protect our army from serious injury and that the injured will heal. Still, all those dead bodies lying around the Garden is a clear reminder that even with the healing properties there is no certainty in avoiding a permanent end.

Plus, the healing properties will also work against us, mending the monster as we try to take it down.

It's been nearly an hour since the voltway opened and everything is still calm in the Garden. Beth has been noticeably quiet. This monster scares her, though if anyone can take care of it she can. She has escaped its wrath three times, once all on her own.

"What are you thinking, Sis?"

She sighs. "I'm trying to decide how to tell you something."

"What?"

"Remember when Mom, and Ruth, told you to not look at the monster?"

"Yeah?"

"There was a reason…."

"Syn, Beth!" Crystal appears from out of nowhere. "Lundy hacked Masie's password and restored the system in the sewers! He thinks he can shut this thing down!"

I smile for the first time in ages. "That's great news!"

Crystal runs to tell everyone and I return my attention to Beth. "What were you trying to tell me?"

"I was talking about the monster, but it doesn't matter now."

She couldn't have been more wrong.

The crackling electrical currents encircling the voltway have sped up, like someone pushed the fast-forward button on a VCR. Beth stifles a scream and I watch, horrified, as a gigantic three-toed reptilian foot and scaly leg slips through the voltway.

BOOM!

The pointed heel gouges into the ground, sending a wave of horrified gasps throughout our army. The other leg follows.

BOOM!

The monster's familiar hair-raising screech vibrates throughout the Garden to announce its arrival. Sitting on its haunches, it towers at least five stories above us. At this close proximity, I can't even see above its kneecaps. Instead, I am facing two oversized green and brown scaly legs, thicker than a century-old oak tree.

It turns its back and thunders away, chasing the two Creeper birds that are circling overhead.

BOOM, BOOM, BOOM!

Just one of those feet could flatten any one of us into a pancake—immediate death, a permanent end. Jagged spikes on its tail, which could knock over a house with a single swipe, carve a craggy path across the grass.

The monster leaps into the air, its puny, unproportioned wings, unable to assist liftoff. The ground quakes like we're at the epicenter of a failing fault line when the monster lands. Rat-Girl screams, pushing and shoving her way through the petrified crowd, and runs in the other direction.

Lucky for her, the monster is still interested in the Creeper birds. It leaps again, flailing its grossly thick arms miles off the mark. Its arms are human-like, except for the bone dagger protruding from the wrist. The sight of that turns my stomach. But when Rat-Girl's screaming has the monster whirling in our direction, I can't keep my eyes off its face.

*Mom, Dad, what the hell did you do?*

This is a face I recognize all too well.

The face of the monster…*is my own.*

# Chapter 49

# THE MONSTER WITHIN

MOUTH GAPING, THE MONSTER'S razor-sharp teeth are primed for their next meal. It draws an immense breath, puffing out its furry chest. The mass of fur patterns from a countless array of animals vibrates with its next ear-piercing screech.

BOOM, BOOM, BOOM!

Mangled Masie bodies are trampled as the monster pursues Rat-Girl. Beth buries her face against my shoulder as the sounds of Rat-Girl's screams become unbearable. Handfuls of our army disperse, scattering in every direction to who knows what fate.

It doesn't look good for Rat-Girl. My stomach turns as she trips and rolls to the ground. The monster is just two strides away from her and scoops her up as if she truly were a rodent.

I cannot tear my eyes away from the horrific scene. Rat-Girl flails about in mid-air and a deathly silence befalls the Garden as the monster spears her with a bone-dagger protruding out of its foot. Its jaw drops like a cobra's and its fangs crunch into her belly, tearing her in half and downing the first bite with one gulp.

Beth's legs go weak and I have to hold her up. The monster tosses the rest of Rat-Girl's bloody, limp body into the air and catches it in its mouth. Before I can blink, her remains are in the belly of the beast.

Aside from Cole's gruesome end, I have never witnessed anything so horrific. The Creeper birds have flown the coop. The Creeper dogs have scampered behind the trees, whimpering. They know they are no match for this thing. None of us are.

"Charge!"

*Or are we?*

Hogan has aimed a military-grade machine gun at the monster. He shoots with intense rapid fire and it staggers backwards, blood spewing everywhere. Others fire their guns at the monster too.

*Maybe this thing can be taken down!*

But to our dismay, the monster shakes off the attack and roars with triumph. Hogan drops his weapon and runs like hell, the monster on his tail. The monster's chase wreaks more havoc on the Garden.

BOOM, BOOM, BOOM!

Cabins are smashed by its giant three-toed feet. Trees and bushes are demolished, sideswiped by its tail as it closes in on Hogan. Hogan zigzags back and forth because there is no way he can outrun the monster.

Ahead of him, Greeta is prepared to face it. She is holding the flame-thrower that Cole used to kill most of Maya's family. Greeta aims high and the monster is hit by the inferno. It has been stunned. When the flames die down, its scales are singed and sparks are sizzling in its fur. Will it fall?

No, it will not.

It roars, leans down, and clenches Greeta's head in its mouth. Before I can cover my eyes, the monster spits Greeta's headless torso to the ground. Upon impact, the flame-thrower shoots flames at Butterfly-Man. The monster watches, intrigued as poor Butterfly-Man howls and squirms, and drops to the ground in a charred heap.

Now, to my horror, Beth is sprinting for the monster while it's distracted. She stretches out an arm like she's on a pitcher's mound, but she's not holding a baseball. She's holding a grenade.

"You're not close enough!"

She pulls the pin anyway, whips the grenade, and dives for cover.

BOOM!

The monster is unfazed by the blast. And even worse, now my sister is in the crosshairs of the monster, racing for her life.

BOOM, BOOM, BOOM!

"Beth!"

BOOM, BOOM, BOOM!

Three more grenades are hurled from the trees. Despite being injured, the monster isn't slowing down. It's rapidly catching up to Beth.

"Faster!"

The monster bends down and the mane of fur around its long neck grazes the grass Beth has just run across. That jaw, which could tear through an elephant, is ready for another meal. Spiked teeth snap shut just as Beth skids across the grass like she's sliding to home plate.

*She's safe!*

Beth leaps to her feet and bolts in my direction. "Go go go!" she yells to Snake-Man, who is crouched beside one of the few remaining cabins, waiting for the monster, with another grenade. The monster's massive tail swings into the cabin as it charges after Beth, sending Snake-Man flying. He drops the grenade in mid-flight and collides with a tree trunk just as the grenade explodes.

Bullet-ridden and singed from fire and grenade hits, the monster swings for Snake-Man and misses under a barrage of gunfire from the treetops. It staggers.

*It's going down!*

No, it isn't. It lifts its bald head to the sky and roars another battle cry.

Head down like a charging bull, the monster rushes at the attackers in the trees. It whacks its tail against the tree trunks, knocking three Creepers to the ground. Lobster-Man is left dangling on a branch by one of his claws. The monster sees his next light snack, ready to be plucked from a tree.

I cover my eyes but cannot avoid the blood-curdling scream that follows. Numb with shock, my arms drop to my side. Lobster-Man's claw is still caught on the branch. That's all that's left of him.

Beth rejoins my side in utter disbelief, struggling to catch her breath. "This thing just won't die!"

So much blood, death, and carnage.

"Is that…?

"Oh no."

Lundy is lurking in the trees behind the monster with a shotgun. He hammers a stream of bullets into the monster's back. "Die, you son of a bitch!" The monster spins, blood spewing from its mouth. Lundy drops the gun.

"He's out of bullets!"

Beth is already on her way back to ground zero.

"Beth, wait!"

Lundy has a grenade. He yanks out the pin and pitches it, but the monster whacks it away. It lands at Mitchell's feet! He turns to run but doesn't get very far. With no shell to protect him, Mitchell is severely burned.

Beth takes my arm. "It's staring at you!"

My heart is pounding. Is it aware that we share the same face?

"Maybe it won't come after you."

"It saw my face in the valley and almost had my bony body for breakfast."

"Right."

I hadn't realized it, but we are slowly inching backwards. The monster seems to be smirking, as if amused. It puts one foot in front of the other, slowly advancing in our direction. Without warning, it charges like a rhino.

BOOM, BOOM, BOOM!

We bolt, zigzagging between bushes and around trees, while the monster tramples those same bushes and trees mere seconds later. I trip and plough into a bush behind Cole's old cabin. My shirt is caught on a branch.

"Rip your shirt!" Beth shrieks.

The monster is looming over us from the other end of Cole's cabin, watching me try to free myself. It enjoys the thrill of the hunt.

Beth tears me loose, yanking me to my feet. "Run!"

"No! Get ready to take cover."

The monster has crept from behind the cabin, stealthily moving in for the kill. I can't believe what I'm about to do. I pull a grenade from my pocket and whip it as hard as I can. It lands short, rolling a few feet in front of a bush. The bush moves, and Flint climbs out from between the branches.

*He was supposed to be watching from the staircase platform!*

"Move, Flint! I run towards one confused boy, and one live grenade.

"No!" Beth grabs my arm and I shake her off.

I won't let her stop me. There are only a few seconds left to save Flint's life.

*Even if it means ending mine.*

I charge forward and am about to jump on the grenade and shelter Flint from the blast when someone shoves me to the ground.

"Roy?"

Roy scoops up the grenade and hurls himself at the monster's feet just as the grenade explodes. The blast sends Beth, Flint and me flying backwards.

After a moment, I sit up. Beth checks that Flint is okay, while everyone else peers at the monster that's sprawled on the ground.

Rose runs to Flint, and then spots the burnt body at the foot of the fallen monster.

"Roy?"

My eyes cloud over with emotion at the sound of her distress. She fearlessly dashes past the monster and over to her husband. He is burnt and bloody. One leg and both arms are lying on the grass, detached from his body. Part of the right side of his head is missing. I don't understand how he can still be alive. Rose lifts Roy's face to hers and whispers his name.

He opens his eyes and smiles weakly. "Rose. I…love you. I am…so sorry…."

And then he is gone. A sacrifice to save his son.

We all wait, hopeful that the Garden's healing properties will bring him back. They don't. Clearly, the damage to his brain is comparable to being shot in the head.

The wailing monster trembles occasionally. It's bleeding profusely. The explosion hit it hard, but not hard enough.

Larry approaches with a machete in his trembling hands. "It's not dead."

"And soon it will heal," says Beth wryly.

She is right. As time passes, the healing properties will save the monster.

Larry's grip on the knife loosens. "I know what has to be done. But I can't do it. I'm sorry."

Beth takes the machete from him.

We trudge past the grieving family. Rose is wracked with sobs, cradling Roy's lifeless body. Flint watches sadly, with the odd nervous glance at the wailing monster.

*If only there was a way to transport this creature back through the voltway.*

Beth leans over the monster with the machete raised. "The only way to bring peace to this world is to end its life."

"I can't let you do this."

"It needs to be done before it regains strength."

The monster's eyes—my eyes—are gazing at Beth like a sad puppy. Beth's eyes well up. The machete doesn't move.

I can't let my eleven-year-old sister do this. The monster shares my face and that blade must go through its brain to end its life forever. Beth will have night-mares for the rest of her life.

*As will I.*

"Hand me the blade."

"No. I can do this."

"I know you can, Beth. You can do anything. But you shouldn't do this. I won't let you."

She gazes at me quizzically, through tearful eyes.

"I know. I feel sad when I see a dead fly, and weep when a bird has an injured wing." I gesture to the destruction around us. "But this is all because of me. Mom and Lily are dead. Roy and all those Creepers are dead, because of me."

"This isn't your fault."

"It is my responsibility to protect the Garden. And to protect my sister."

I hold out a hand for the machete, meeting Beth's pleading eyes with determination. "You have always had my back. This time, I insist on having yours."

Beth is biting her lip. She doesn't stop me from sliding the handle from her hands. I kneel beside the monster's head and raise the machete. While looking into its eyes, into my eyes, it occurs to me that this could be the machete that was used to murder my father. I clench my teeth with that memory. My anger rises like an inferno and with one long, raging battle cry, I lift the blade. It comes down hard. Blood spatters my face as the blade slices through flesh and crunches through skull before it thrusts into the monster's brain like a knife through cold butter.

I lower my shaking hands to the monster's throat. My entire body feels chilled, as if I'm in an ice locker. There is no pulse and no breath. No life. I collapse on the grass and wail like the beast whose life I just ended, in what is surely the darkest moment of my life.

Chapter 50

# BREATHE IN

MY PARENTS INADVERTENTLY CREATED A Frankenstein monster that had my face—a monster that is
now dead by my hands.

A part of me died today as well—my innocence.

Beth and I lie next to the monster's body for a
long time, holding hands. I am grateful for each
breath, for the blue sky above, and for the support of
the Earth beneath me. I close my eyes, thankful for
having the strength to get through this, and for being
able to take care of my sister. I am grateful that neither
she nor I are among the fallen.

When I open my eyes, Beth is gone. I sit up,
glancing around for her. It seems like the entire
surviving population of the Garden has encircled me.

"Your sister went to the house." Larry lends a
hand to help me up.

"Oh. Thanks."

We stroll for a good distance to be clear of the
monster's resting place. Larry's company is comforting. He kindly leaves me with my thoughts, waiting
until I am ready to speak.

"How many died?" I finally ask.

"Eight counted so far," he says gently.

I sigh.

"Some were badly injured, but they're healing quickly," he adds. "They will—"

"Did you know?" A familiar voice interrupts our conversation.

Larry leaves me to face Rose. Flint stands a couple feet behind her, his eyes moist.

"We met Roy in the valley. He begged me not to tell you that he was still alive. He said he didn't want to hurt either of you anymore."

Rose shakes her head slowly, and draws Flint close. "I don't understand any of this."

I try to make eye contact with Flint, but he turns his back. My heart is breaking.

"I am so sorry." Those are all the pathetic words I can muster.

"You must leave the Garden, Synthia," Rose says sadly. "And never return."

"You have my word."

Despite all the pain I have caused everyone, Rose lovingly touches my arm as I walk away.

There are certain people I want to see before leaving. While strolling through the Garden, I am horrified by the damage the monster has caused. Residents are mulling about their cabins in shock, assessing the damage. Some watch warily as I make my way to the pond. The once idyllic bridge has been snapped in half.

The person I'm looking for is in the Square. Fawn is nestled up against the well, resting her chin on her knees.

"I don't want to see you," Fawn says.

"I…just wanted to say…"

"…that you are sorry?"

I say nothing.

"By admitting those women into the Garden, you chose one friend's life over the lives of all your friends here. My daughter was your age. Now she is gone forever." Her voice falters. "Can you imagine her terror as she fell to her death?"

"I…"

Can you imagine knowing you're going to die?"

"Fawn…I…"

"I don't care that you meant well. You always mean well. You're a kid still figuring things out. So was Lily. There is only one thing you can say that will give me any semblance of peace."

There is a long silence. Fawn is waiting for me to say what she wants to hear, and I comply.

Like I just finished telling Rose, I give her my word that I will leave the Garden and never return. I then leave her to mourn the loss of her only child.

The house doesn't appear to have sustained damage beyond that caused by Masies crashing through the roof. If the house came down, the Garden's healing properties would likely be lost along with it. And adding to that, I don't know if there would be a way for us to get home.

Lundy is sitting at the top of the back steps, hunched over, his cheeks resting in his hands.

I sit down beside him.

"I set up a lightway for you and Beth in the carport. You can go home when you're ready."

"Thank you."

"Sure." He continues to sulk.

I place one hand on his shoulder. "I know how you're feeling."

"Yeah. You probably do."

"You're in mourning. And if that isn't hard enough, you blame yourself for the deaths of others."

Lundy still won't look at me.

"Do you blame me for Lily's death?"

He casts sad eyes upon me. "I blame them."

"I blame myself."

"You shouldn't."

"I'm responsible for all the terrible things that happened in the Garden."

"You tried to save a friend. I shot that woman point-blank, in cold blood."

"That had consequences you could not have foreseen. You blame yourself. Trust me, I get it."

"How do you get over it, Syn? The guilt and the loss."

"You don't. You know what my mom told me?"

He raises his eyebrows.

"She told me to get over myself."

"She *would* say that." He almost breaks a smile.

"My mom was right. No matter what we have done, we can't change the past and deprive ourselves of a future. Even if that future may be without people we love because of our actions. We can only move forward and do better next time, and try our best to live without constant guilt. That guilt will hold us back from our true potential to do good."

"That's profound, Syn. You rehearse that?"

"Lundy, I'm guessing you're thinking about returning home? Even if it means facing charges for a murder you didn't commit?"

He doesn't deny this.

"If you think that's the best way to move on, I won't try to convince you otherwise. But if you want to stay here, stay. No one blames you. Only Beth and I saw you shoot Masie. For all anybody knows, the contingency plan took effect because all the Masies died when they fell."

Lundy ponders this.

"Decide how you will make a difference in the world, wherever you choose to be. That's all you can do."

"Perhaps I'll stay here and help fix up this place. Make the Garden the best it can be for the humans and Creepers who live here."

"Lily would have liked that."

"How are you moving forward, Syn? What are you going to do?"

"I'm going home."

* * *

Beth and I are standing in front of our parents' graves, holding hands. We hold the silence for several minutes, reflecting on good memories and letting go of bad ones.

"I'd like to say something."

"Of course," says Beth.

"Mom, Dad…I love you." I glance at my sister. "And I promise to take care of Beth."

"And I'll take care of Syn," Beth chimes in. "I'll miss you both so much."

Then I say something I didn't expect. "I forgive you."

"Wow, Syn. I'm proud of you."

She shouldn't be proud of me because I wasn't being honest. I do love my parents, but I could never forgive them for experimenting with and killing children, or the other murderous things they did in a twisted attempt to save me.

When I first came to the Garden, I learned that the healing properties keep the souls of the dead here. Their last semblance of life remains, so in a way they will never truly die. My parents, Lily, and everyone else who has died since Mom fixed the healing properties remains here in spirit. Giving my parents closure feels like the right thing to do.

"It's time," I say.

Lundy, Jeremy, Larry, and Crystal are waiting at the carport to see us off.

"Beth is going home ahead of me," I announce. "After a month with no meds, I will be in rough shape when I leave the Garden. In about thirty minutes, Beth will have an ambulance waiting to take me to the hospital."

Crystal scoops Beth into her arms and they share a long goodbye hug. Beth calls goodbye to the others over Crystal's shoulder, grinning because Crystal is squeezing her so tightly.

After Beth has gone, I have some time to kill before the ambulance will be ready, and decide to take one final stroll through the Garden. I try not to focus too much on the damage. My thoughts turn to the time I first woke up in this beautiful paradise. How I made new friends and found peace I had never known. I was a healthy person for the first time in my life.

I amble alongside the pond and down to the Square, where I first met Lily. I bounce my feet on the spongy path through the bog, then make my way to the spiral staircase. While I'd like to see the bird's-eye view of the Garden once more, I won't put myself though the trauma of being in the place where Mom and Lily's lives were cut short.

The current state of the Garden is heartbreaking. It will take time for everyone to heal and rebuild. For now, I choose to focus on the good memories. It's time to walk back.

As my path nears the lightway, I am shocked to see Luke walking towards me.

"Luke!" I rush into his arms.

"It's good to see you, Kiddo."

"I've missed you."

"I'm sorry I couldn't be here to help you guys."

"Why are you here now?"

"I came to bring you home, and to the hospital. When Ebby tracked me down after she returned from the Garden, I took the next plane home. I've spent a good part of the last month visiting your garden, hoping a lightway would appear so I could come and help you!"

"There were many times I thought of you."

"You saved my sister's life," Luke says. "Now it's my turn to save yours."

All I can do is smile.

The friends who saw Beth off are still gathered in the carport, while Hogan and Mitchell have chosen to wave goodbye from a distance. Nell is standing beside Lundy, but is avoiding eye contact with me. She blames me for her best friend Lily's death and is eager for me to leave. In the distance, Maya is hanging from a strand of web that's attached to a tree branch. I can't see her face clearly, but I swear she is hiding a smile.

"This isn't goodbye," Larry says. "You'll come back to visit, right?"

Crystal and Jeremy bow their heads.

"Oh," he says, frowning.

"Luke, you go first, okay? I'll be right behind you."

He salutes me.

I take one last deep breath with healthy lungs, savoring the fresh Garden air. I wave to my friends and they wave back. With a lump in my throat, I enter the light and leave the Garden for the very last time.

# Chapter 51

# BREATHE OUT

I ALMOST DIED THE DAY I returned from the Garden. Yeah, I know. What else is new? Aside from barely escaping my adventures there and in other alternate worlds, my cystic fibrosis has threatened to cut my life short as far back as I can remember. Lengthy hospital stays have monopolized my childhood. Antibiotics and other treatments have saved my life on a number of occasions, along with the love and support of family, friends, and health care workers, and my own fighting spirit.

Just as Beth had promised, an ambulance was waiting when I exited the lightway. She and Luke were not taking any chances. Beth took my backpack, and Luke carried me to the gurney where the paramedics were waiting.

It wasn't surprising that in less than five minutes my lungs were burning. I coughed up more blood than ever before. The doctor noted that my lung function was so low, and my lungs were so infected, it was a miracle I was still alive. That miracle had to be the treatment I was given in the *Futurama* world.

I spent six long months in the hospital, my home away from home. Ebby, Jon, Luke, and of course Beth, have been my rocks. Crystal even came to our world for the first time to visit me. She enjoyed using her chameleon-like camouflage abilities to prank the staff and cheer me up.

When not visiting me, Luke, Jon, and Ebby are helping to rebuild the Garden. Lundy has left the voltway open so the residents can expand their horizons, since there is no longer a monster rampaging through the valley. Luke is helping them build cabins in the valley, where they can grow different types of food because of the warmer climate.

Oh, did I mention that Luke has a serious boyfriend? He met Tony Gonzales in Haiti during his Habitat for Humanity project. Tony is a former army medic and a seriously great guy. He moved to Redfern to be with Luke, and works as a paramedic at Redfern Memorial.

Luke has become a lifesaver in more ways than I could have imagined. The court has granted him status as our legal guardian. We have no other family and I'm not yet eighteen (or capable of being granted guardianship of Beth with my regular hospital stays) so Luke stepped up. The judge was hesitant to hand the responsibility over to such a young guy, but the alternative would be foster care. Beth and I begged the judge to allow Luke to become our guardian on a trial basis, also noting that my eighteenth birthday was just months away for good measure. It's worked out great so far. Tony moved in and I have to say that I love my new little family.

That is a lot of good news for a girl who has spent six months fighting for her life in a hospital. But as is most often the case, with the good also comes the bad. And the bad news was quite the blow. Even though I recovered well, I lost my place on the waiting list for a lung transplant. People think that the sicker a patient is the more likely they will move to the front of the line. The truth is that many factors determine whether a person is eligible. The long and short of it is that I have to be sick enough to need a transplant, but not too sick for my body to accept the new lungs.

The odds of me surviving for more than a couple of years without a transplant are not great. But don't think for one moment that I will admit defeat. If I have learned anything from my time in the Garden, it is that when I really put my mind to something, I can do anything.

My medical team has advised me how to get in better shape to be eligible again. No matter how sick I am or how high the odds are against me, I am going to fight like hell to get back on that list. Beth will not lose the only relative she has left. The Grim Reaper may already be planning his visit, but my story is far from over. I won't let him and that scythe anywhere near me if I can help it.

* * *

It has been four months since I returned home from the hospital. Truth be told, I've been a bit down. The losses I experienced in the Garden have stayed with me, and I will never get over taking a life. Health-wise, I am not in the best shape, but guess what? I got back on the transplant list! I carry a pager (yes, a pager) with me wherever I go. When they find a donor who's a match, I will receive a page and must call the hospital STAT.

At this moment, I'm lying on my bed studying for finals. Beth and I cleared out the basement and with Luke and Tony's help, set it up as two adjoining bedrooms—our own little suite. Beth is watching a video in her room. Distracted from studying, I try to make out the audio. It's an episode of *Gilmore Girls*, which I told her was a must-see.

I lean against her doorframe. "Good, huh?"

"Eh. It could use some vampires or demons."

I should have known. Beth loves her *Buffy*, *Supernatural,* and *Vampire Diaries.*

I'm caught off guard when my pager beeps. It takes me a moment to realize where the beeping is coming from.

"Is that…?" Beth leaps off her bed as I unclip the pager from my jeans.

I'm numb with shock.

Beth yanks a sheet of paper off my wall and hands me the phone number. "What are you waiting for?!"

I drop my phone.

She swipes it off the floor and thrusts it into my hand. "Call!"

My jittery fingers tap in the number even though it's saved in my contacts. After a few minutes of speaking with a hospital administrator, I end the call.

"Well?"

My legs feel weak. I stumble to my bed and sit down.

"Syn?"

Swimming in a state of disbelief, I manage to spit it out. "I have to get to the hospital. To prep for a transplant."

# Chapter 52

# RED WEDDING

WHEN THE ANESTHESIOLOGIST WAS PREPARING to put me under, I knew there was a chance the transplant would not go as planned. I faded away knowing I may never wake up to see the people I love again.

But I did wake up.

The recovery has been long and hard, and successful. It took almost two months for my new lungs to be functioning almost normally. The wait and struggle were worth it though. Breathing is easy and wonderful—as it was in the Garden—and for the first time I not only feel true freedom, but believe anything is possible.

This doesn't mean that my struggles are over. The cystic fibrosis is not cured. It just no longer affects my lungs. I still have to take two dozen pills daily, in addition to new drugs and antibiotics. Not a problem.

Two weeks ago, Beth, Ebby, and I returned from a camping trip in Oregon to belatedly celebrate my eighteenth birthday. It was wonderful to explore, hike, and even paddle a canoe without having to worry about every breath.

My new lungs are foreign objects in my body and there is a possibility my body could reject them. I take anti-rejection meds to reduce the chance of that happening. Most cystic fibrosis patients survive after a lung transplant for at least five years, some ten or more. After that, they could be in line for another transplant, but that is not a certainty. Who knows? Maybe there will be a cure before I have to worry about that.

The original prognosis was that I wouldn't live past twenty. With my eighteenth birthday just behind me I would happily take five more years, if I am lucky enough to get them. Ten years would be a dream. For now I can enjoy life, spending time with my family and friends.

Every breath is a gift.

I'll never know the identity of the person whose lungs saved my life. I was permitted to write their family a letter to tell them how thankful I am and hopefully give the death of their loved one some meaning—to know that in some way they continue to live within me.

There is something else to be happy about. Luke and Tony are getting married! Today!

Of course I insisted that they have the wedding in our garden. It's their home too. They invited a modest group of forty. Ebby, Beth, and I went all out planning a great night.

* * *

I'm standing under the arbor by the pond, adjusting a floral arrangement, when Ebby rushes down the aisle all flustered. Her cheeks are bright pink.

"The caterers were supposed to be here twenty minutes ago. I'm freaking out!"

"It will be fine," I reassure my friend, placing an arm around her. "Better than fine. Everything will be perfect."

I was right. The ceremony was beautiful. Luke and Tony's friends are great. Both their families are here, except for Luke's ignorant homophobic father. His loss.

The band is awesome. Luke and Tony twirl off the dance floor and glide past me. "Hey, Beautiful!" calls Luke. "Save me a dance, okay?" He winks and we share a private joke about the time his sister Ebby tried to set us up.

"You bet!" I call, my voice breaking up suddenly. My throat is dry and scratchy, probably from shouting over the loud music.

I'm feeling kind of tired, but a dance with Luke would be special. I watch the happy couple cut loose and feel so happy.

The tall buttercream wedding cake at the center of the dessert table is calling to me. It's the tastiest cake I've ever had. I've already eaten two pieces and don't want to be a pig. Perhaps I'll have another piece later, when nobody is looking. For now, a sip of water should fix that tickle in my throat.

Everyone is having a blast on the dance floor and I decide to go relax where it's quiet. It's nearly midnight and this has been a long day. Plus, I haven't seen Beth in a while. Maybe she is hiding out in the garden.

I stroll alongside the pond, admiring the lantern lights the guys strung up this morning. They set a truly romantic mood for the evening. The garden is deserted.

A couple of men are folding up rental chairs in the reception area. There is still no sign of Beth.

As "Under Pressure" is booming in the background, I lift my head and inhale the fresh evening air, gazing happily at the stars. My breath is cut short when a sharp pain stabs my chest. I double over, clutching my chest, hacking my lungs out. I'd almost forgotten what this feels like. Each cough feels like another stab in my chest.

I'm startled to see that I've coughed up a spatter of blood into my palm. The chest pain intensifies and I can hardly draw a breath. Gasping for air, I drop to my knees, still clutching my chest.

*No! Not now…Not today.…*

# Chapter 53

# SYNTHIA'S CHOICE

I'M LYING ON MY BACK, hoping the starry September sky won't be the last thing I ever see. One of the guys who was collecting chairs is kneeling beside me, shouting.

Before I know it, Luke and Ebby are crouching over me. Their mouths are moving but I can't hear what they are saying. Tony arrives with Beth and Jon. There's a crowd of hazy faces watching me.

"Our limo is out front, Syn," Luke says slowly. "I'm going to lift you. We'll take you right to the hospital."

Beth and Ebby are crying as Luke lifts me into his arms. He carries me through the garden where moments before I was the happiest I have ever been. The band stops playing.

*I've ruined their wedding.*

As Luke lays me on the seat, Beth is screaming. "No, take her back to the Garden!"

The doors are slammed shut and the driver revs the engine.

I cough and blood spurts on Luke's beautiful tux, and on his face. He doesn't even blink.

"It will be alright. We'll be at the hospital in a few minutes."

"Syn, keep your eyes open, okay?" Tony says, in full paramedic mode.

"This is bad. We have to go back!" Beth shouts hysterically. "Take her to the Garden. Whether she wants to go or not."

"Beth." Luke shakes her shoulders to knock her out of her panicked state. "Beth, listen to me. We have to get your sister to the hospital."

"No, the Garden!" Beth's face blasts into my reality again. "She has to go back to the Garden." Beth is sobbing uncontrollably. "Why isn't anyone listening to me? Syn, tell them!"

"Your sister can't talk right now." Luke leans over me. "Syn?"

*I should have told her.*

I nod solemnly, and Luke's attention returns to Beth.

"She can't return to the Garden, Beth. The lightway is closed to Syn forever. That Masie woman who helped you, who was on your side? Syn asked her to permanently lock her out of the Garden. Like how Masie Winters was locked out by your parents."

"Why?!" Beth screams.

Beth's, Ebby's, Luke's, and Tony's faces turn blurry, and are replaced with the faces of Mom, Dad, Lily, and Janna. It's like they are waiting for me to join them. My mind turns to mush. Nothing makes sense. There is just one coherent thought as reality fades.

*I should have had another piece of cake.*

# BETH

THE DOCTOR SAID THAT A powerful infection had weakened her lungs, and that it hit her hard.

The memorial wall I am facing displays names of deceased patients whose families donated to the hospital in their memory. The birth year and year of death are displayed on plaques. Luke is standing next to me.

"Some of them are so young," I say. "Here's a boy my age."

"Life can be cruel and unfair."

"Here's Syn's friend, Janna." I sigh. "It would have been so easy to return to the Garden. We could have built a house in the valley and lived a healthy life. Our Garden friends could have visited us."

"Your sister was determined to be true to her word," Luke says. "She promised the people of the Garden that she would never return. Asking that woman…"

"…Ruth…"

"Right. Asking Ruth to permanently close the lightway to her was the only way your sister felt she could keep her promise. Syn knew that if she got really ill one day, she would be tempted to return to the Garden, and that you would insist."

She was right. I just wish she had told me.

Syn had a chance to turn her back on mortality. Most people would have jumped at such an opportunity, especially those with a chronic illness. I know Syn had her reasons, but I don't get it. She has always had such a passion for life and yet she decided to forsake her own.

And what about me? When she asked Ruth to lock her out of the Garden, did she do it on a whim, or was it something she had thought about for some time? I may never know.

I lean against Luke and he wraps an arm around my shoulder. Dr. Freeman is approaching, and a rock is growing in the pit of my stomach.

"Beth…"

Tears begin to stream down my face.

"It's okay. I have good news."

"G-good news?"

"Your sister is awake. She's asking for you."

# Chapter 54

# LIFE GOES ON

WHEN I OPENED MY EYES in the hospital, I thought I was in the afterlife. I never took that stuff seriously but when everything went dark in the limo, I didn't expect to open my eyes again. I thought my story was over.

Fearing rejection of my new organs, doctors kept me in an induced coma and put me on a ventilator. They fought the infection with antibiotics.

I can't put into words how happy I was to see Beth and my friends again. I am perfectly aware that one day my luck may run out. My body could still reject my new lungs at some point, or there could be other health issues.

The choice I made in the Garden makes it impossible for me to return. And though I experienced some regret during the limo ride to the hospital, it was the right decision. Not only because of the pain I caused the Garden residents, but because I want to have as normal a life as possible, with no magical land to escape harsh realities. Beth accepts my choice even though she doesn't understand it.

I'm strolling through our garden, hand in hand with my sister. The garden behind our house was my oasis long before I woke up in the *other* Garden.

I'm set to make up my finals and graduate from high school next week. After the break, I'm going to take part-time college classes in the evenings. I'm not certain what I want to do—perhaps something along the lines of social work, helping others who have had hardships in their lives. Having grown up without my parents and living with a terminal illness, I can relate to people who are struggling.

While I feel fantastic today, breathing in the crisp, fresh air, I realize my life could be cut short at any time. I want to have some real-life experiences. Go on trips. Spend time with my new family and my friends. I joined a dragon boat team with fellow organ recipients, and love it.

Right now, I'm enjoying a perfect moment in my favorite place with my favorite person. If I die tomorrow, I'll die happy. But I don't plan to die any time soon. I'll continue to take care of myself and fight to live as long a life as possible.

Life is short. I accept that mine may be shorter than most, and will take one day at a time. My vow is to live each day to its fullest, as if it could be my last, because I am finally able to accomplish that simple task that's been a struggle for most of my life. Now, I can honor those two words I have often whispered to myself with great longing:

*Just breathe.*

# Acknowledgements

I am beyond thrilled you are holding the final book of the Garden of Syn trilogy. It has been an incredibly fun ride and I am appreciative to so many who supported me on my journey.

My parents, Shelley and Perry Seidelman, and my sister Sara Solomon have been my biggest cheerleaders since day one. Their support and feedback were instrumental to the writing of the trilogy.

A huge thanks to Tracey Lutz for your wonderful constructive feedback and your support. As well, thank you to Lillea Brionn for your helpful feedback.

A big shout out to Dr. Mark Gelfer for reading my early drafts and for answering my questions on medical issues. Any mistakes are my own.

Thanks to my fantastic editor, Davina Haisell, who tirelessly helped me present the final draft you hold in your hand.

Once again, I want to thank the cystic fibrosis community for supporting and embracing the series. I hope I have given those with CF and other terminal or chronic illnesses a hero to root for and that there is satisfaction with the conclusion of Syn's final adventure in the Garden. Of course, Syn Wade is a fictional character who has adventures in a fantasy world. I have nothing but admiration for those battling cystic fibrosis and other chronic and terminal illnesses in real life.

Finally, I want to thank you, my readers! Thank you for taking a chance on a new author and reading this series. Thank you for your ratings and reviews, your blog posts, shares and likes on social media and for recommending the series to others. Writing fiction is my dream job and you have helped bring that dream to life. I hope you will continue to read my books for years to come. I can assure you I have no shortage of ideas and characters and will be writing novels for as long as you continue to read them.

# About the Author

When Michael Seidelman was growing up, his passions were reading, watching movies, enjoying nature and creative writing. Not much has changed since then.

Having worked in Online Marketing for over ten years, Michael now works full time as an author.

Michael was born in Vancouver, BC Canada where he continues to reside.

You can learn more about Michael Seidelman at www.michaelseidelman.com. You can also follow him on Facebook, Twitter, Instagram and GoodReads.

This story is fiction but cystic fibrosis is very real.

70,000 children, teenagers and adults in the world suffer from the disease. While treatment is far above what it once was, there is still no cure. Let's help find one.

Please check out these sites for more information on cystic fibrosis and how to donate to help find a cure.

Cystic Fibrosis Foundation (US) - https://www.cff.org

Cystic Fibrosis (Canada) - http://www.cysticfibrosis.ca

CF Trust (UK) - http://www.cysticfibrosis.org.uk

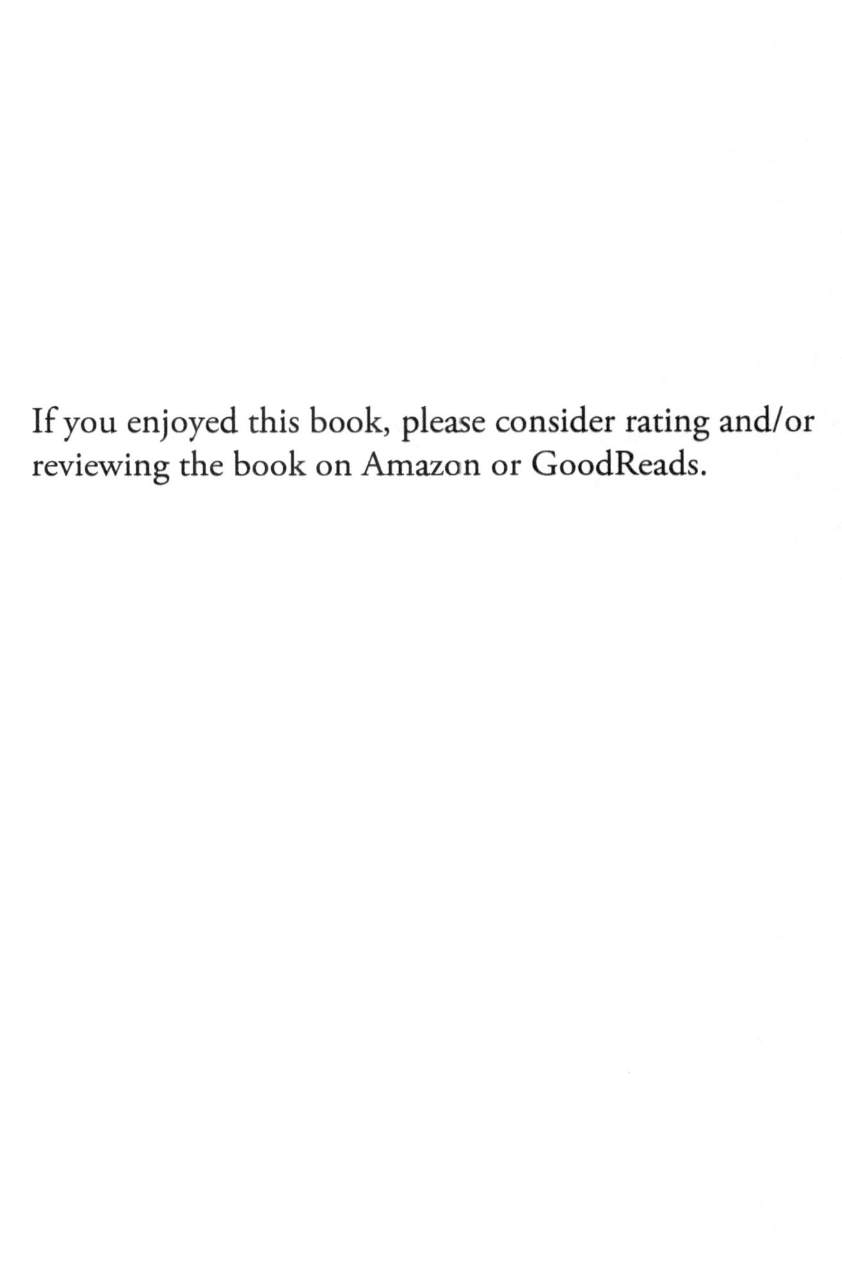

If you enjoyed this book, please consider rating and/or reviewing the book on Amazon or GoodReads.